ALSO BY PAUL J. TEAGUE

Morecambe Bay Trilogy 1

Book 1 - Left For Dead

Book 2 - Circle of Lies

Book 3 - Truth Be Told

Morecambe Bay Trilogy 2

Book 4 - Trust Me Once

Book 5 - Fall From Grace

Book 6 - Bound By Blood

Morecambe Bay Trilogy 3

Book 7 - First To Die

Book 8 - Nothing To Lose

Book 9 - Last To Tell

Note: The Morecambe Bay trilogies are best read in the order shown above.

Don't Tell Meg Trilogy

Features DCI Kate Summers and Steven Terry.

Book 1 - Don't Tell Meg

Book 2 - The Murder Place

Book 3 - The Forgotten Children

Standalone Thrillers

Dead of Night

One Last Chance

No More Secrets

So Many Lies

Two Years After

Friends Who Lie

Now You See Her

PROLOGUE

Morecambe 2006

'This will be some front-page spread,' Rory Higson said with a smile, as he set up the photograph which he hoped would have copies of The Bay View Weekly flying off the shelves that week. 'I'm so pleased we finally managed to get you all together in the same room.'

'Well, let's make it snappy, shall we?' said Edward Callow. 'We're holding an informal meeting as soon as you're finished, then I have to get back to London for an important vote in the House of Commons.'

Unusually for a newspaper reporter, Rory was intimidated by his local MP, a man with a blunt, dismissive and impatient manner. For a man like Rory, who'd found contentment in the seaside resort, bringing up his family and becoming an integral part of the local community, the drive behind the accomplishments of this group of men was phenomenal. As he positioned them around the table, ensuring the composition of the photograph would be worthy of a front-page spread, he considered how well they'd done in such a short time.

There was no doubt that Edward Callow ruled this roost. He and Harvey Turnbull clearly held all the power, and the others were deferential to them. Even Mason Jones, the pompous ass of a head teacher who'd presided over the opening of one of the town's biggest infrastructure projects for some years, took his place in the pecking order behind Edward. That must have come hard for a man used to being surrounded by people who had to listen to him. He was head of the brand new, purpose-built, award-winning secondary school serving the young people of the More-cambe Bay area; but he and everybody else of influence in the town knew that it would never have happened without the joint efforts of this group of men.

'Can I get you a cup of tea or coffee?' a friendly voice asked from behind him.

Rory turned around. It was Isla Thomas. Rory knew her husband Richard and her son, Philip; both worked on the boats, and he'd interviewed them for the newspaper several times since the cockle pickers tragedy in 2004. They were familiar with the bay, its dangers and vagaries. Both were an authority on the area, after living there so long.

'Hello, Isla, thank you, I'd love one.'

Isla smiled at him and headed off to the kitchens.

'Get me one too while you're there love,' Harvey Turn-bull shouted. 'White, two sugars. Don't make it weak as piss, or I'll send you back to make it again.'

'Where's that idiot Rex Emery?' Edward cursed. 'I asked him to have the filter coffee machine ready for us, and it's still gurgling away over there like it's got an upset stom-ach. Is it too much to ask to have everything ready for our meetings? We hire this room often enough.'

As if sensing he was needed, Rex Emery darted into the room, a pile of freshly laundered tablecloths in his arms.

'My apologies, Mr Callow. We had a problem checking out one of the guests this morning, and I was late getting the room set up. That coffee should be ready by the time Mr Higson is finished.'

'If he ever gets finished...' Edward muttered under his breath.

'Okay,' said Rory, 'I'd like Mr McMillan in the middle, seeing as he's just landed that movie tie-in. Congratulations, by the way. You must be proud.'

Barry smiled.

'You might say that,' he said. 'If the producer can land a big name in the lead role, I'll be even happier.'

Fred Walker was the strong, silent type. He was big, broad, and was carrying too much weight. As the head of a hugely successful construction company, Walker still prided himself on mixing the first batch of concrete on any new building site. It was a move which won the respect of his staff; he was a boss who still lifted a shovel and had cracked hands where the cement had dried his skin.

He moved slowly and deliberately into his seat on the left. Mason Jones, a small man, sat to his side, obviously feeling diminished by Walker's frame. It was a difficult one for Rory to manage. Walker was like a bag of bricks compared to the other men, who'd never had to pick up a wheelbarrow or wield a spade to make their living.

'I tell you what, Mr Walker, if you could swap places with Mr Mason, that will balance out the photograph better.'

Rory decided that he'd use the circular table to his advantage, shooting the picture with a bias to the right-hand side; that way, Fred Walker wouldn't seem too dominant

4 PAUL J. TEAGUE

and it might avoid making Mason Jones look like the weaselly little toad that he was.

Isla stepped in with a tray and hung back while Rory placed Edward Callow and Harvey Turnbull to the right of Barry McMillan.

'Bring that over here, darling, I'm parched,' Harvey Turnbull said.

As Isla set the small teapot, jug of milk and cup down, Rory distinctly saw Harvey Turnbull push her. Tea splashed out of the teapot on to the table.

'Jesus, watch what you're doing!' he yelled at her. 'Can't get the bloody staff,' he scoffed.

Mason Jones laughed nervously, Edward sneered, and Barry McMillan looked uncomfortable as he shuffled in his chair.

'I'm so sorry,' Isla said, her face colouring with embarrassment.

'Emery! Get your arse in here,' Edward Callow shouted out.

Rex Emery came back into the room, responding to the summons.

'If you can't find decent staff to serve us while we're meeting in your dump of a guest house, we'll find somewhere else.'

Rory noticed Isla and Rex exchange a glance. Rex looked like he was about to say something, but he held his tongue. The atmosphere was so unpleasant. And it was Edward Callow and Harvey Turnbull who made it that way.

He had a lot of time for Fred Walker and Barry McMillan, having encountered them frequently on the local reporter circuit.

Barry always seemed charming and patient at his

increasingly less frequent local book signings, and Fred Walker understood the value of a decent front-page photograph whenever he put on his old overalls and posed with a spade and wheelbarrow.

Rory continued to frame the shot while Isla cleared up the spillage. As she leaned in to wipe up the last of the tea, he was sure Harvey Turnbull moved his hand to the top of her leg and ran it along her thigh. The look on Isla's face and the way she jumped seemed to confirm his suspicions. Rory paused a moment, wondering if he should say anything. He decided against it; he was there to take a photo, not put right all the wrongs in the world.

He began to fire off camera shots as the men sat chatting, checking the light and making certain he was happy with the composition.

'Not using digital yet?' Rex Emery asked, as he brought in a replacement tray of tea for Harvey Turnbull.

'I have one in my bag, but I still go belt and braces. I prefer film. The editor has different ideas, unfortunately; he reckons it's the future. I'm not so sure.'

As Rory settled the men for the final, formal shots, Isla and Rex re-arranged a few items on the bar, making sure that the backdrop wasn't spoilt by any dirty glasses or sodden beer mats from the previous night's guests. The click and whirr of Rory's camera could be heard throughout.

'Any chance we can get some of these photos?' Harvey Turnbull asked. 'It's not every day I get to appear on the front page of the local newspaper with a bunch of tossers like this lot.'

There was polite laughter from the others, apart from Edward Callow, who was frowning.

'Besides, my missus would love one of these. She's gone

all posh now we've moved to Hest Bank. You'd think she was the Queen of Morecambe, the way she behaves.'

'Yes, no problem. I've taken lots of informal photos while you've all been chatting, and I'll be happy to send some prints your way once they're developed. The newspaper won't use them all.'

Rory called for their attention now, ready to take his shot. He fumbled for the digital camera in his bag, although he resented using it, convinced that it would be the death of quality photography.

'Okay gentlemen: one, two, three... thank you. I'll take a couple with this camera, then a couple on film.'

He snapped away. By the looks on their faces, you'd think they were just a pleasant bunch of guys who were all doing well in their lives. He wouldn't deny them that, but he'd seen some things that unsettled him that day.

Rory had known Edward Callow since he'd worked in the planning department at the town council. That role had brought him the contacts and influence that had taken him all the way to being an MP in London. There was no denying he was an ambitious and powerful man; but was he wielding that power wisely? From what Rory Higson witnessed on that day, he wasn't so sure.

He took his final round of shots, then told the men they could relax.

'Thank fuck that's over,' Harvey Turnbull said.

'Emery, I want a word with you before you disappear,' Callow called out. 'I need to ask you about renting a room here...'

Callow lowered his voice as he ushered Rex across to the bar to speak confidentially.

'I'll be off now, gentlemen,' Rory announced, pleased to have completed the job. 'That picture will run with a full-length article in next week's paper. It'll be quite some photograph. Years from now, people will look at that picture and wonder who all those powerful men were and why they were gathered here like this. You're making history, gentlemen; you're changing people's lives in this town.'

CHAPTER ONE

Morecambe - Present Day

'We have to tell the police about Lucia. We need to get them involved now, Will; we can't leave our daughter out there on her own. Whatever trouble she's got herself into, we have to help.'

'I'll call her,' Will said, frowning. He still didn't look well, and Charlotte was concerned. The earlier assault on him at the guesthouse had been violent and, strictly speaking, he ought to have been checked over by doctor, even though he seemed to be recovering well. She was strapped into a stretcher, ready to be loaded into an ambulance at any moment, and they were taking her away from her precious family. Even though she was worn out and exhausted, she still had to protect her children.

She watched as Will took his phone out of his pocket and keyed in Lucia's number. She could see from his face that it had gone straight to voice mail.

'We'll load you up in the ambulance in a minute. Are you about ready to go?' the ambulance man asked.

'Yes, just one moment if you don't mind. I need to sort out one or two family matters,' Charlotte replied.

'Where are you taking Charlotte and Olli to?' Will asked.

'Lancaster,' the man answered. 'They've better facilities there.'

'I'm exhausted,' Charlotte said, 'but I'm not hurt. I'm scratched, bruised and cold, but once I can stop this shivering, I'll be fine. Mind you, I do feel sick; I took in so much sea water out there, I reckon I'm half mermaid now.'

Will smiled.

'I want to get off this trolley and look for my daughter. DCI Summers is over there. Call her across, will you? We need to tell her about Lucia.'

Will did as he was asked. Charlotte could tell he wasn't right, but he was the only family member still available. Even she knew that it was best to get a check-up at the hospital. She'd stay no longer than she had to, but she and Olli had had a near miss out by the jetty. She thanked her lucky stars that they'd made it, all too aware that they might have been grieving for their son if she hadn't got there in time.

Ahead of her, Olli was being moved into a separate ambulance. He was in shock, and they'd struggled to get his temperature under control, but he wasn't in imminent danger. Charlotte desperately wanted to reach out and touch him, to reassure him that everything would be okay. It stung her to see him out cold on that stretcher, when there was nothing she could do to help.

Then she realised there was something that she could

do; she could get herself cleared at the hospital, then go out looking for her daughter.

'Hi Charlotte,' DCI Summers said. 'Will's updated me on your daughter. Do you have any reason to believe she's in harm's way? Who might be with her?'

'That's it. I just don't know. She was with this guy who had a purple Mohican haircut, and she seemed comfortable with him. But she's been acting up recently; something's going on. I don't think this guy is a good influence, let's put it that way.'

'How old is your daughter now?' DCI Summers asked.

'Seventeen,' Charlotte replied.

She detected a change in DCI Summers' attitude.

'Look, just because she's above the age of consent, it doesn't mean some guy can help himself and do whatever he wants!' Charlotte said, thinking DCI Summers should know better.

'I didn't mean it that way; it's just that... well, the level of trouble that she might be in is different at that age. She's almost an adult.'

'But she isn't yet, is she?' Charlotte challenged. 'And it's not like her to go missing.'

'I'll need to speak to you about what happened to Edward Callow outside the Midland Hotel,' said DCI Summers, changing the subject. 'And about the young woman in the West End who was almost strangled. I know you didn't do any of those things, Charlotte, but you don't have to be a detective to see this has something to do with you and your family. The sooner you tell me what it is, the sooner I can help you.'

Charlotte glanced at Will, but he still seemed disoriented. He had to hang on in there; he might have sustained a concussion. She ran through the things that she could reveal to the police. The attack on Will, Olli's abduction, whatever had happened to Lucia; this was all safe territory.

What about the videotape? Would that implicate them? Did it even matter any more? Rex Emery had said the video contained evidence of whatever had gone on all those years ago at their guest house. There were still copies available, and Will had to get his hands on one.

'Let's get the hospital out of the way first, and then I'll be happy to answer all of your questions.'

She spoke the words, but she still wasn't entirely sure that she meant them. With Daisy Bowker also sniffing around, the house of cards could easily collapse. Once her daughter was safe—once she had all her family with her—only then did she and Will have to consider telling the truth.

The thought of it made her light-headed; the promise of being unburdened of their lies was intoxicating. Yes, the time was coming. But first, her family had to be safe. If she had any leverage left in relation to Bruce Craven, she had to retain it. And she still wasn't certain that this was even connected with Craven. It was just that everything had a funny way of coming back to that psychopath of a man.

'We'll need to speak to Olli too,' DCI Summers continued. 'You do realise he'll be interviewed as an adult now he's eighteen, don't you?'

Charlotte hadn't given it a thought. Would he say something that dropped her and Will in it? She'd have to trust that he wouldn't.

'I'll catch up with you at Lancaster Infirmary,' DCI Summers said, then walked off to speak to one of the attending police officers.

'Do you think she knows?' Charlotte whispered.

Will was acting as if he was miles away.

'What?'

'Do you think she suspects us?' Charlotte asked.

Will seemed to snap back into full consciousness.

'She knows we're not involved. And we're not; we've done nothing wrong. Remember, it was Jenna who killed Craven; George is our witness.'

Charlotte had forgotten all about George.

'What did he say about his cancer?' Charlotte asked.

'It's not good,' Will said. 'He's undergoing tests. They're struggling to figure out what's wrong with him.'

'Did he tell Isla yet? She suspects already.'

'No, not yet. He was asking for my advice on whether it's better to wait or tell her straight away. He wants to spare her as much pain as he can.'

'Poor George. They've had so little time together. What did you advise him?'

'I told him I couldn't say. Let's face it, you and I never discussed Bruce Craven for thirty-five years. We're hardly the best people to advise anyone when it comes to hiding secrets in a marriage.'

'How long does he have, if the tests confirm he's ill?'

'At his age it's more likely to be months, not years.'

Charlotte was overcome with a wave of sorrow. The thought of losing George was unbearable, and even worse for Isla. They'd barely known the two of them a year, yet already they were an integral part of their family life, like a third set of grandparents. Then she remembered Will's discovery.

'You told me Isla was in that photo with the men. She must have been lying to me when she said she didn't know Rex Emery.'

'What?' Will asked. It was as if his mind was lagging

behind. Even when she was fighting fatigue, Charlotte knew she was more alert.

'Isla,' Charlotte repeated. 'The picture you were putting together. Isla must have been aware of those men?'

'Yes,' Will finally replied, as if he were processing the information bit by bit. 'I haven't spoken to Isla about it yet. She and George are at the guest house now. I asked them to stay. Or rather they volunteered to stay. I told them to sleep in one of the empty rooms if I'm back late. We'd be lost without those two.'

He appeared to have forgotten their conversation about George already. For a moment Charlotte considered leaping off the trolley and sending Will to the hospital instead. But she was the one caught up in the incident; she'd have to tolerate the medical checks, the paperwork and the inevitable questioning by the police.

'Will, I need you to do something while they take me to hospital. I haven't told you the full truth, and you'll just need to trust me when I tell you this. Rex Emery, the chap who used to own the guest house, is on the run from prison. I know where he is. He's in a boarded-up shop just along from the dilapidated church on the street corner, close to The Boardwalk. Find him and tell him you need to secure one of the videos tonight and place it somewhere safe. He'll understand what you're talking about. Tell him I sent you. Take care. He might think you've come to harm him.'

Charlotte couldn't believe those words were coming from her mouth. She ran a guest house in a seaside resort; all this talk of murder was a million miles away from her everyday life.

'Near the church, you say?'

'Will! I need you to focus.'

Charlotte was getting frustrated. The ambulance staff were coming to collect her, and she was running out of time.

'I heard you,' Will replied.

'Then I need you to go back to the guest house and wait for Lucia. Try to find out why Isla lied to me about Rex Emery too. I want to know how she's involved. And whatever you do, don't walk into Daisy Bowker's trap; do not say anything about Bruce Craven. That woman doesn't miss a trick. She'll catch you out if you're not careful.'

'I've got it,' Will said. 'Look, I've got my phone booster with me; do you want it? It'll charge your battery in case Lucia calls. Here, plug it in. I'll get over to Lancaster as soon as I can, to check in on you and Olli.'

The ambulance crew came to collect the trolley, one at either end.

'Okay, my darling, it's time to go. You'll catch your death of cold if we leave you out here any longer.'

Charlotte let her head sink into the small pillow. She would have to let it go and rely on Will, at least for now. Even though he wasn't quite right, he was their only chance. He had to find out what was going on.

CHAPTER TWO

Morecambe - Present Day

Will was being pulled in so many directions that he didn't know what to do for the best. It was just past eleven o'clock, and the thought of Lucia being out there terrified him. But before he could take action, he needed to see his wife and son taken to safety. His head was pounding, and he'd had difficulty with his vision since being struck at the guest house. If he hadn't been the only remaining member of the family capable of getting that video, he'd have jumped up into the ambulance himself.

Charlotte's trolley was pushed into the ambulance and the doors were closed. Will had already checked on Olli. His son was frightened, exhausted, sore and grateful for being saved in the nick of time. Thankfully his life was no longer in danger; he just needed to be cared for by medical staff and get some rest.

Will had looked up the symptoms of concussion before he met Charlotte on the sea front, having realised he wasn't well. In fact, he'd just been about to telephone for a taxi and get himself checked at the town's hospital when Nigel Davies had called to alert him about what was going on at the stone jetty. As he watched the ambulance join the traffic on the main road, he resolved to keep going. He was still walking and still had clarity of thought; he could get himself assessed later.

'Do you need to speak to me before I go?' he asked DCI Summers before leaving the area.

'Have I got your mobile number?' she asked.

'Maybe not,' he replied. 'Let's add it to your phone, just in case. With Charlotte in hospital, I'm your best port of call if you find Lucia. You promise you'll let me know the moment you find her?'

'I promise,' DCI Summers said. 'We've alerted the patrol cars and specials who are out, and Pubwatch also got a notification too. There's been nothing back from the hospitals either, which is always a good sign. Look, it's Saturday night, when we have more officers on the streets than on any other night. If she's out there, we'll find her. At the moment she's just about the only other member of your family who's not in a hospital. That's a positive, isn't it?'

Will nodded. She'd seen the dressing on his head, but he wasn't ready to talk about that just yet. Lucia was his priority. And so was the videotape that Charlotte had asked him to secure.

'Okay, thanks. If you want me, you know how to get to me. I'll take your business card so I can phone you if I need to.'

She handed one across and he entered her number into his phone.

The rescue scene was all but clear now, with just two

uniformed officers, DCI Summers and a man and a lady from the lifeboat crew still in attendance.

'Thanks for your help tonight,' he said, putting out his hand to shake theirs. 'I don't know what we'd have done without you.'

He walked off towards the main road, trying to remember the instructions Charlotte had given him. Rex Emery was the guy's name. Somewhere near the old church, she'd said. He began to walk towards the West End of the promenade, looking closely at the shops as he did so, checking each one to see if it was boarded up. There were more boarded up than he'd have liked to see; he didn't recall that many when they were students visiting the town in the eighties.

He pulled out his phone to try Lucia again. There were no new messages. He dialled her number. Voice mail again; he was sick of hearing her message.

'Lucia, it's Dad. It's ten past eleven now, and we're worried sick about you. The moment you get this, call me. The police are looking for you, so if you see a police officer, tell them who you are and they'll help you. Whatever it is, Lucia, we can fix it. Love you, kiddo, take care.'

Will could see the spire of the abandoned church up ahead. He sat on a wall and called the guest house. George answered.

'Hi George, great, you're still up. Charlotte and Olli are fine. I don't suppose Lucia called, did she? She hasn't come home already?'

'Sorry, Will, no sign of her and no calls. Well, just a few prank calls. Saturday night messing about, I assume.'

'What kind of calls? Could it be Lucia?'

'Just silence when I answered. I'm sure it's only kids.'

Will didn't share his confidence.

'I'll get back to the guest house as soon as I can, George, but if you and Isla want to take that vacant double room, help yourselves. We'll pay you of course.'

'I won't hear of it, Will. You know how much we love your family. We'll stay as long as you need us; I've brought Una here for the night, but I promise I'll keep her out of the kitchen. There are a couple of guests still up in the lounge. She's gone down a storm with them.'

'I'll bet she has,' Will replied, imagining the scene.

'You know that thing we spoke about earlier...'

George had lowered his voice now.

'I've decided that I ought to tell Isla. It's only fair. But I'll wait until things have settled down. We need to talk about what happened too. I'm the last person who can vouch for you and Charlotte about that night at the holiday camp. I may need to leave a letter or a recording. When I die, if I die, there will be nobody left to protect you, if Jenna Phillips decides to blame you for Bruce's death. He's still buried out there. They'll find him if they have to.'

'We'll speak later,' Will replied. 'But don't worry, I won't say anything to Isla.'

He paused a moment, wondering if now was the time to raise it.

'Does Isla ever talk about working at the guest house when she was younger, George? Has she said anything about those men who were murdered?'

Should he tell George about the image? He'd concealed it in the drawer beneath the bookings laptop which was kept in the hall. He decided against it; it was probably best discussed face to face.

'She doesn't say much about those early days. But she doesn't seem very concerned about the deaths of those men. She hates that Callow fellow, I can tell you that much. But she's cagey about those early days, and I don't push her. Maybe she has secrets of her own that she doesn't want to share?'

Having pieced together the photograph, Will suspected that she probably did. He thanked George again for helping them out with the guest house, then ended the call. He stood up and headed for the church, seeing its dark silhouette looming up ahead. There were no shops before the church, just a row of B&Bs, much like their place. The church itself looked abandoned. Was this the one Charlotte meant? She'd definitely told him it was a shop, yet those across the road were all occupied. He began to curse. The pounding in his head didn't help. It was much more than a headache; the pain seemed to run deep beneath his skull.

He crossed the road to the next row. This was where The Galleon used to be, the place where they used to go for tea before catching the last bus back to the holiday camp. He was overwhelmed by a sudden surge of nostalgia and affection for the years they'd spent together. Even after all this time, he'd do anything to keep Charlotte safe.

There was a shop with a full skip outside. Large sheets of chipboard, sodden with the rain, were nailed across the door and window frames. Will walked up to it, looking for police officers or passers-by. They'd already got into trouble for breaking into the abandoned theme park, and he didn't want to find himself in trouble with the police again.

As he got closer, he could see that one of the chipboard panels was loose; it had been worked free of the frame. This had to be the place. Somebody had got in there and left themselves an easy exit. The chipboard was still loosely attached with a few rusted-through nails. It pulled off the fastenings easily.

Will stepped into the building through the window

frame, keeping hold of the chipboard sheet. He lit up the torch on his phone, placed it nearby and manoeuvred the board back into place, matching the holes to the nails and securing it once again.

Behind him, there was a movement, a scratching sound. He turned, picked up his phone and pointed its beam around the room. The place was a deathtrap. There were missing floorboards all over, piled-up boxes and building materials covered the floor, and to the side of him was an old bookshelf. Something moved near his feet. In the dark shadows, he couldn't work out what it was, so he pointed the flashlight at it.

Will let out a loud shriek. What he'd thought was a loose length of electrical cable turned out to be a rat's tail, right next to his foot. Rats terrified him. He turned to get away, put his foot in a gap between the floorboards and stumbled. As he reached out his hand to grasp the bookcase in a vain attempt to steady himself, the rat jumped up at him, and Will and the bookcase came crashing to the ground. He thrashed wildly at the creature, trying to brush it away from him.

As the bookcase toppled on to him, several boxes behind it fell to the ground, shaking the wooden joists. There was a loud thump from the room upstairs, and then a large lump of plaster broke from the ceiling overhead, crashing down and smashing across Will's head.

CHAPTER THREE

Morecambe - 1984

The Battery was busy that Saturday afternoon. The Shrimps were playing an away game in the Northern Premier League, and that meant the pub was busy with fans who hadn't made the trip to see the game. It suited Edward Callow. Nobody would give a damn about his conversation with Mason Jones. They'd all be preoccupied with their home team's performance on the pitch.

Edward couldn't care less about the football, but he knew that it was the secret to winning hearts and minds in the town, so he feigned interest and kept on top of the team's fortunes, more for conversational ammunition rather than anything else. He preferred to play different games, and they tended not to involve kicking balls around.

He nursed a pint of Thwaites bitter, tuning in and out of the conversations nearby. He'd bought an extra pint in anticipation of Mason's imminent arrival, but the froth on the top had had time to settle now, and Edward was already half-way down his own glass. Where the other drinkers were content to talk about their families, their jobs, the demise of the local football team and the quality of the pint served in the pub, Edward's mind was constantly scheming and plotting.

He had big plans. Morecambe was a seaside town in decline, but as he worked in the planning department, he could see that there were many lucrative opportunities coming up. These weren't small-fry house renovations or hotel refurbishments. Edward's eye was on the multi-million-pound contracts, the type of projects which made men rich.

He'd fallen into planning. It wasn't his first love. But as he'd learned the ropes at the Town Council, forged relation-ships and seen how things worked, he'd soon spotted an opportunity.

But he couldn't do it alone. And that's why he was currently nursing a pint of beer which he didn't particularly want to drink, in a pub he'd rather not have been in, waiting for the unlikeable head teacher to show his face.

Edward noticed a man at the bar, drinking on his own. He was a young man—mid-twenties perhaps—built like a fighter, with tattooed arms. Leaning against the bar, he was confident and self-assured. He gave out an aura which made the other men step around him, appearing brooding and quiet, aloof from the football talk and content in his own company. He clocked that he was being watched. Edward averted his eyes. This man was of interest to him, but he didn't want to engage just yet.

Behind him, a younger group, probably students, were getting rowdy. They didn't have the world-weary demeanour of the other drinkers, who were there for refuge from the old week that had passed and the new week that was rapidly approaching. It was a mixed group of eight—five boys and three girls—and it looked like one of the students was a little more cocksure than the others, telling jokes and making everybody laugh. This student was annoying the hell out of Edward, and he could see that the man at the bar had also noticed it.

'Sorry I'm late; you know how the traffic is on a Saturday.'

Mason Jones sat opposite Edward and offered a handshake. Edward knew his sort well and was primed to redress the balance of power.

'When I fix up meetings, I expect them to begin on time,' Edward began. 'If you want the opportunity to be on this consortium, I expect you to behave in a certain way.'

Edward observed Mason's face. This had not landed well. As a secondary school head teacher, Mason was used to ruling the roost.

'As I said, it was the Saturday traffic. I had a bit of a job parking...'

The students at the table behind them let out shrieks of laughter, and half the customers turned to see what the fuss was about. They were beginning to get on Edward's nerves. He noticed the man at the bar slowly turn round, assessing the group and watching the young chap at the centre of all the hilarity.

Edward's hand moved to his inner jacket pocket. He pulled out three Polaroid images and dropped them on the table in silence. Mason looked at them, realised what they were and snatched them up.

'Jesus Christ, Edward, what the hell are you doing? Where did you get these?'

'There are more where those came from,' Edward said calmly.

The look on Mason's face said it all. The balance of power had just shifted considerably in Edward's favour. Mason Jones would think twice about being late for a meeting again.

'What the hell do you want? I thought we were going to talk about the building contract for the school. This looks more like blackmail.'

Edwards looked straight at Mason without flinching.

'This entire proposition is about business,' he began. 'I won't make moral judgements about what you get up to with some of your sixth form students. They're over the age of sixteen, as far as I can tell from those photographs. But this is what I'll be using instead of a contract. All that paperwork seems too formal and unnecessary.'

Mason's face was white. He looked like a teenager whose mum had just walked in on him, sitting with the lights dimmed to create a conducive atmosphere and a copy of Playboy in his unoccupied hand.

'Who took these?' Mason asked.

'You don't need to know, and I'm not telling you. But this is the beginning of what I hope will be a productive and lucrative business arrangement. So long as you honour your part of the deal, I'm happy for you to continue whatever it is that you like doing with these girls. You deliver this building contract to our consortium, and I'll make you a rich man. You can forget your crappy head teacher's salary. We can rule this town if we get this right.'

Edward was playing his own good-cop, bad-cop routine. Mason Jones was bordering on narcissism, which was fine by him. It gave the little shit the self-confidence and longing to make this thing work. The truth, which Edward would admit to nobody, was that he needed to land this deal for the new school, or his own aspirations of power and riches would be dead in the water.

A beer mat clipped the top of Edward's ear as it came flying over from the table of students. It narrowly missed the top of Mason's pint and landed at his feet. Edward glared at the group.

'Sorry, mate,' the cocky student shouted. 'I didn't mean that to hit your table.'

Edward grimaced.

The man at the bar walked over.

'Are they bothering you?' he asked.

'A little,' Edward replied. 'But it's okay, that lad apologised. Thanks for your concern.'

The man with the tattoos returned to his place at the bar and ordered another pint. He'd attracted attention from two women standing nearby, who were giggling together.

'So, you've got the names I asked for?' Edward asked.

'Yes, everything,' Mason replied. 'Home addresses too, for every key person who's involved in awarding this contract. Dare I ask what you're going to do with it?'

'Think of yourself as a facilitator,' Edward told him. 'This information is essential to the wellbeing of our project. And you reckon it's not going Fred Walker's way?'

'The thinking is that it's too soon for Fred Walker to take on a project of this scale. The bid was considered good; he just doesn't have the track record yet. It's a huge project. It has to go right and be delivered on budget.'

'This is good, Mason, thank you. I see you as a crucial part of this consortium. You have access to all the great and the good of the town through the school, as well as all the relevant contacts and influence at county level. They needn't find out what you get up to in your spare time, and as long as you restrict your little hobby to youngsters above the age of consent, you won't have me on your case. After all, we have to draw the line somewhere, don't we?'

Mason shuffled in his seat. Another beer mat came flying in their direction, landing just behind him this time.

'Sorry mate, it was an accident!' the cocky student shouted.

The man at the bar turned slowly and walked across to the table of students. Without a pause, he picked up one of the empty beer glasses, smashed it on the edge of the table, grabbed the cocky student by the hair and held the smashed glass to his eye.

All conversation in the pub stopped as everybody watched what was going on.

'You're disturbing these two men,' he said. 'Apologise and fuck off out of here.'

A patch of dampness spread across the groin of the student's jeans. His friends looked stunned at the sudden threat.

'I'm sorry, I'm really sorry,' the cocky student said, snivelling and terrified.

The man released his grip from the student's hair and placed the broken glass back on the table.

'I'll pay for the glass,' he called to the landlord who was watching from the bar, one hand on the phone receiver in case the police were required.

In complete silence, the group of students got up, put on their jackets and filed out of the pub. The chatter picked up again, largely in support of the eviction of the noisy group.

Bloody students, acting like they own the place.

That's taxpayer's money they're drinking. They should be studying, not disturbing the likes of us.

Edward was impressed. He needed a man like this; intimidating, calculating and threatening. His own personal strength was in the more cerebral side of the operation.

The stranger approached them.

'They won't be bothering you again, gentlemen,' he said. He thrust out his tattooed arm towards Edward, who grasped it readily and shook it.

'Bruce Craven. Pleased to meet you,' the man said.

CHAPTER FOUR

Morecambe - Present Day

It took Will several moments to figure out what had just happened. His head felt like it had been smashed with a demolition ball, his eyes were sore with plaster dust, and the bookcase was pressing down on him. He could just about see the light from his phone, which had fallen to his side. The rat was still scuttling about somewhere in the room. There was also a thumping sound nearby, as if someone was coming down the staircase.

'Is that you, Rex?' Will called, rubbing his eyes, which felt like they were congealed with plaster dust.

The footsteps stopped. Will guessed the person was pausing, considering what to do next.

'It's Will Grayson, Charlotte's husband. She sent me to see you.'

'How do I know it's you?'

The man sounded scared.

'I know about the video you gave to Charlotte. That's what I need to speak to you about.'

Will was struggling to get his sight back. He needed some water to rinse away the burning sensation in his eyes; fat chance of that in a derelict building.

'Is her son safe?' came the voice, slightly more confident now. Will heard the creak of the staircase.

'Our son,' he replied. 'Olli is our son. And yes, they're both safe. It seems I need to thank you for your part in that.'

'You know I'm on the run, don't you?' Rex asked. 'The police are looking for me. Edward Callow is after me too.'

'It looks like we're all in danger, myself included. You don't have a bottle of water, do you?'

Will heard Rex approaching and sensed he was picking up the phone at his side. Through his blurred vision, he could see the beam had now been trained on him. Rex was obviously checking his identity.

'Damn, are you okay?'

Rex's voice relaxed, and he set about pulling the bookcase off Will.

'The ceiling fell down on me and I've got plaster in my eyes.' Have you got anything to rinse them out?'

Rex touched his hand with a plastic bottle.

'Careful,' he said. 'I found it thrown into a bin, but I misplaced the cap. Don't waste it. It's all I've got.'

Will took the water, poured it into his free hand and splashed it at his eyes. It gave instant relief, even though his eyes still felt red raw. Gradually, his vision cleared, and he could get a proper look at Rex Emery in the muted light given off by his phone.

Will rinsed his eyes one last time, blinking away the final pieces of dust, then handed the rest of the water back to Rex.

'You look terrible,' Rex told him.

'I feel terrible,' Will replied. 'I got a blow to the head earlier. I could use some medical attention. But Charlotte almost begged me to come here. If I can stay upright long enough, I need to get my hands on one of the video copies.'

'Did Charlotte tell you she was hiding me in the guest house?' Rex asked.

'No, she didn't,' Will answered. 'But nothing surprises me at the moment. I trust my wife, even if I don't always agree with her. Whatever she was doing, she'll have done it to protect our family.'

'So, your son is safe? That's good news.'

Rex helped Will back to his feet and handed him his phone.

'Yes, but my daughter has gone missing now.'

'Is that down to Edward Callow?'

'I don't know. There's nothing that links her to what's going on yet. But as I said, nothing would surprise me.'

'Why does Charlotte want a copy of the video? The shop is closed now until Monday morning. My plan was to hide and then pick it up when the shop re-opens.'

'I don't think we have time,' Will said, grimacing. 'Charlotte seems to think it's too important; she wants us to break into the shop and get it back.'

'You're kidding,' said Rex. 'I'll be put straight back in prison if we're caught.'

'I'm beginning to think it will be worse if we don't break in. I think the video may be our only leverage now. We can take it to DCI Summers and prove what's going on.'

Rex fell silent for a moment. Will wasn't entirely sure it was the right thing to do. But Charlotte was convinced it was the key to clearing them all, so it had to be done.

'Okay, I'm in,' Rex said at last. 'It's an old-fashioned

shop. The chap who runs it is getting on in years. If it has an alarm though, I'm out. We couldn't risk it. We'd have to wait until Monday morning.'

'Okay, agreed. I wouldn't have a clue how to break into a property, anyway. Can we even get in if it's all locked up?'

There was a scratching on the far side of the room.

'It's that rat again. Can we get out of here?'

Will had no wish to enter into a re-match with the rodent.

'Come upstairs,' Rex said as he moved towards the doorway. 'There are some tools up there. I found a crowbar the workmen have been using to pull the plasterboards off the wooden frames. In fact, I was about to crack you over the head with it, if you were one of them coming for me.'

Will was happy to be on the upper level where he couldn't hear any vermin moving. Rex had created a small den for himself, setting out old newspapers to lie on. The tools were there: the crowbar, a hammer and a bucket.

'I guess we won't need the bucket, but the other two items may come in handy,' Will said, weighing the hammer in his hand. He couldn't believe he was assessing it as a defensive weapon rather than as a DIY tool. How his life had taken a sudden turn. He decided in the end not to take it, it would only weigh him down, and the crowbar seemed more useful for a break-in.

The two men retraced their steps back down the stairs and through the window, taking care to replace the chipboard so as not to draw attention to the fact that they'd been in there.

'This is home now until we get this thing sorted,' Rex said.

'Where's the shop?'

'Not far. I suggest we use the back alleys rather than walk along the sea front. There's less chance of being spotted.'

Will looked at the crowbar in Rex's hand. Keeping a low profile was the best bet.

It took ten minutes to find the shop, which was located on the ground floor of a corner terraced house, well away from the town centre. That was a blessing; with nobody about, it would make their break-in much easier. They stood in the darkness of the alley opposite, figuring out a plan of attack.

Will examined the shop front, still struggling to see properly. He couldn't tell if it was caused by the blow to his head or the plaster dust.

The sign read *Vern's Videos*, making Will wonder if the owner's career choice had been determined by the first letter of his Christian name. The paint on the shop's fascia was faded and peeling in places, mirroring the demise of the technology in which Vern must have placed his faith during the early eighties.

'Looks like we're going in through the front door,' Rex whispered, having reached the same conclusion as Will. 'You keep a lookout while I force the door. I can't see any sign of an alarm, can you?'

'No,' Will replied. A surge of adrenalin was tearing through his body. This was crazy. If they got caught, he could lose his job as a lecturer.

They crossed the road. Will looked through the window, searching for the telltale sign of movement sensors flashing in the darkness.

'Let's do this,' he whispered.

Rex moved forward, his hands on the crowbar, ready to

force it into the small gap between the door and the frame. Will watched as he pushed it in, and the door creaked wide open. Somebody had got there before them.

CHAPTER FIVE

Morecambe - Present Day

The two men looked at each other.

Further along the street, a young couple could be heard chatting as they walked home.

'We'd best go inside,' Will suggested.

They ducked through the doorway, pushing the door shut behind them, then stood in silence in the darkness, waiting for the couple to pass. Their lively conversation made Will pine for Charlotte. The easy, relaxed company and enjoyable chatter were what he'd always loved about their relationship, from that first meeting on the double-decker bus as they headed for a day off in Morecambe.

'Okay, they've gone,' Will said. 'What next?'

'The counter is over here. He put the videos at the back somewhere.'

'You took a bit of a risk handing them over like that, didn't you?'

'Not at the time,' Rex replied, a little short with Will. 'I had a copy of my own before I left the shop. I gave it to your wife so she could save your son, if you remember.'

'Sorry, you're right, I apologise. Ignore me. My head's not in the right place. This is all new to me...'

'You think I'm used to this?' Rex asked.

Will decided to keep his mouth shut. He meant Rex Emery no harm and he was willing to take him on trust, based on Charlotte's judgement.

There was a groan from behind the counter.

The two men froze, tense and alert.

They heard a second groan. The voice sounded frail and elderly.

'That's Vern,' Rex said, rushing toward the counter. Will followed him.

The light from the streetlamp opposite the shop door was bright enough for them to see what was going on. They were met by the sight of Vern lying on the floor, dazed and confused. Will knew the feeling.

'Vern, are you all right?' Rex asked, kneeling at his side.

'They hit me,' Vern answered. The shadows behind the counter made it hard to get a good look at him, but Will thought he sounded old, post-retirement old.

'Have they taken the videos?'

Vern struggled to raise his head and get a proper look at who he was talking to.

'Are you the man who came in earlier with that pretty young girl? You wanted the copies made, yes?'

'That's me,' Rex replied.

'What was on those videos?' Vern asked. 'Whatever it was, they weren't leaving without them.'

'Let's get you up off the floor and on to a chair,' Will suggested. 'Shall we turn the lights on, Rex? We can't keep bumbling around in the dark.'

'Can you take me through into the kitchen?' Vern asked. 'I'd like a drink of water, please.'

They helped him up and guided him through the narrow door at the side of the counter. It led to a hall with a staircase to the upstairs accommodation, plus a small toilet and a functional kitchen on the ground floor. It had once been a house, but Vern must have turned it into a shop several years ago. The place smelled musty and damp, as if it was in dire need of some love.

With the kitchen light on, Will was able to take a proper look at Vern. He reckoned he was at least seventy years old, possibly even nearing his eighties. His mind flicked to Isla; what was it about their generation, that made them carry on working well into their old age?

'What happened?' Rex asked. It was fairly obvious. Vern had a large, egg-shaped bump on his forehead.

Will found a glass, filled it with water and handed it to Vern, who drank it like he'd just spent the past three days in a desert.

'Three men,' he said, 'Three of them came in. I've been running this shop since the days of Betamax videos. We opened thirty-seven years ago, in my fortieth birthday year, and it's kept food on my table ever since. Can you believe that in all this time we've never been broken into? I'll have to give it up now. My son's been warning me for years that I need to retire. But what else would I do? My darling wife died when I was sixty-five. What am I going to with myself, go into a home and sit in an armchair all day? Most of my old friends are dead now, and this place is what keeps me sane.'

Will wanted to give Vern a hug. How long would he and Charlotte be immune from the sort of events that he was describing? They weren't a million miles away from that stage of life. It got depressing if he stopped to think about it too much.

'Can you describe the men?' Rex asked, much more on the ball than Will.

'One of them had a strange voice,' Vern said, thinking it over. 'I've only ever heard something like that on the telly before. He was rasping, as if he'd had an operation or throat cancer. It sounded painful when he spoke.'

Will tried to recall his own attack. He'd been struck from behind, and they'd been waiting for him. He couldn't recollect any voices.

'Did you get a good look at them?'

Will could see that Rex Emery had picked up some useful tricks whilst spending time in police custody. He was persistent with his line of questioning.

'It was dark,' Vern continued. 'I heard a noise downstairs, as if I'd left a video playing in one of the TVs. It sounded like men's voices. I didn't bother turning the lights on. I just thought it was me being absent-minded again. That's when they hit me. They knew exactly what they were after. They wanted your videos. They were horrible people. I almost got away with leaving the master copy in the copying machine, but the man with the funny hair remembered to check—'

Will was immediately alert.

'What kind of funny hair?'

'Well, these youngsters do all sorts of weird and wonderful things to their hair these days. I couldn't get a proper look at him, because of the poor light. But his hair was all sticking up, like the fellows you see in the old cowboy films. What do you call it?'

'A Mohican haircut?' Will suggested.

'That's the one,' Vern answered. 'He was pierced too,

everywhere. Ears, nose, eyebrows... it's a wonder they can find any space. I think he had tattoos too; all round his neck.'

'We need to find this man. He's the one responsible for Lucia's disappearance...'

Will stopped. Although his mind was still deathly sluggish, he'd just made the connection. If the man with the purple Mohican was involved with the video, that meant Lucia hadn't disappeared randomly or got mixed up with an unsuitable boyfriend; she was in as deep as the rest of them. A rush of unfettered panic rose through his body as he imagined the terrible harm that could come to her.

'Are you okay?' Rex asked. 'You look terrible, even worse than you did in the dark.'

'I think they've got my daughter,' Will said. 'This guy with the haircut, he knows Lucia. They must have been setting her up for this.'

'You said the police were looking for her?' Rex asked.

Will forced himself to conquer his sense of panic. DCI Summers knew they were on the lookout. If she was out there, she'd find Lucia. He had to let them know that this was no regular teenage disappearance. Lucia was in danger.

He began to fumble for his phone in his back pocket. The battery was low. Damn, he'd used the torch too much in the abandoned shop. He'd given Charlotte his charging unit too. Will began to scroll through his contacts, looking for the contact details for DCI Summers that he'd saved earlier.

'How did they know to come here to get the videos?' Rex asked. Will looked up, waiting for Vern's answer.

'Probably the sticker I put on the copy tape,' Vern answered. 'Every time I make a copy tape, I add a little sticker to the video. You'll be amazed at how much business that attracts. People see it and realise there's still some old boy who can fix videos for them.'

'Why didn't I think to check?' Rex said aloud, frustrated with himself.

'It's easily done,' Will tried to reassure him. 'You handed that copy tape over to Charlotte in good faith. Why would you have checked it?'

'I can't believe I was so stupid,' Rex cursed. Will thought he needed to cut himself some slack; they'd all made bad decisions that night.

Will's finger was poised on the dial button to speak to DCI Summers.

'Did they give any more clues as to what they were up to or where they were heading? This is important, Vern. My daughter's safety depends on it.'

'There was one more thing. I only caught the end of it as they were leaving the shop. My hearing isn't so good these days, so I may have got it mixed up.'

'Whatever it is, please tell me,' Will urged. 'Any little piece of information could help Lucia.'

'Well, that chap with the rasping voice swore at the boy with the funny haircut. The language they used was terrible.'

'What did they say?' Will urged, keen to get to the heart of the matter.

'The man with the bad voice told the young guy to shut his effing gob, or he'd do it for him. He was angry with him.'

'What had he said?' Rex asked, equally impatient to see if it was useful.

'I didn't catch all of it, so this may be wrong. But he was laughing about going to sort out some effing bitch and her son at the infirmary in Lancaster I think.'

CHAPTER SIX

Morecambe - 1984

'So, Fred, I think we've got this in the bag. Just the small matter of Councillor White to resolve, then I think we're there.'

Edward Callow studied Fred Walker's face, looking for any giveaway signs that he was having second thoughts. The builder was pivotal to the entire project. After all, what would Edward do, pick up a mortar board and start laying bricks? Chance would be a fine thing. No, his role in this was as the coordinator and manager; he wouldn't be getting his hands dirty in any way.

'We're only a small company,' Fred answered, a worried look on his face. 'I'm not entirely sure we can deliver on a project of this size. It's a school for heaven's sake, and the most we've built to date is a small housing estate.'

'I wouldn't presume to encroach on your territory, Fred, but surely it's just as many bricks just laid in a different order? You need to have a little more confidence in your abilities. If we win this contract, we'll be well on our way to being millionaires. A couple more like it, and we'll achieve something that few people ever attain in this area. We'll be wealthy beyond most peoples' dreams, and we can do it together, Fred.'

The look on Fred Walker's face still didn't suggest that he saw their trajectory the same way that Edward did.

'What if we mess it up, Edward?' he asked. 'We'll never land a contract ever again. My name will be dirt in this town. We'd never recover.'

'I see you're a glass half empty kind of guy,' Edward said, offering a smile. He tried his best to make it sound warm and friendly, but he always suspected he looked like a crocodile. Edward decided to relate to Fred at a more emotional level.

'You'll have to expand the business if that family of yours keeps on growing,' he said. He'd been holding back on this, but Fred needed the extra push. He couldn't do with his main partner getting cold feet, not bearing in mind what Bruce Craven was doing, possibly at that very moment.

Fred nodded his head, and his face reddened just a little. Edward knew he'd hit the mark.

'What is it, three children now?'

'No, still just the two...' Fred corrected him.

In his pocket, Edward Callow had a photograph of Fred's third child. He hoped he wouldn't have to drop it on the table, as he'd been prompted to do with Mason Jones. He preferred his partners to suspect he was aware of their misdemeanours; it was more nerve-wracking for them if they were never sure how much he knew.

Well, Edward certainly knew about Fred's little secret, all seven pounds and six ounces of it. A baby girl, born to Gloria Merryman, the lady who managed the sales office at the small housing estate that Fred had just sold the last house on. Edward believed Fred had installed Gloria in the show home out of his own pocket. There was a certain irony to that. It was a particularly neat solution to a difficult problem. Fred's wife didn't know. They'd been childhood sweethearts, and their love story forged part of the strong family brand for Walker Homes and Construction. It was a family brand that Fred wouldn't want sullied.

Edward had observed early in his career how men with even a little power quickly became intoxicated with it. He hadn't observed it in women, so he was always more wary of them. Fred Walker, the recipient of one or two building quality awards and accelerating his career from a simple brickie to the MD of an impressive local company, simply couldn't keep it in his pants.

The wife who'd known him more than half his life, and who had created the home environment which allowed his business to flourish, no longer provided the excitement required by a man who was carried along by the heady hedonism of status, money and influence. Gloria Merryman would have been out of his league when he was a bricklayer; as MD of a flourishing company, he suddenly became more attractive to women like her, and he could no longer help himself.

Edward was sure a person like Fred would never ditch his family, but like all the other men he knew in a similar position, they always went bad one way or another.

For Mason Jones, it was giving in to his basest instincts. His was a perceived power—over pupils and staff—and a certain amount of influence brought through his connections with local councillors and the great and the good of the town.

Everybody knew that the local school had to be kept on

side when it came to their own youngsters, so it gave Mason clout that he might not have had in corporate life.

Mason walked a fine line; his predilection was for young women who were just on the right side of the legal age of consent. That might have only been creepy or inappropriate, if the objects of his desires hadn't been pupils at his own school. There was no doubt in Edward's mind that Mason used his influence and power to groom more vulnerable pupils. That wasn't his concern. The head teacher would be out on his arse if his weakness ever came to light.

Having observed this behaviour in others, Edward was not so foolish as to deny that the same flaw must reside within him too. He'd scrutinised himself on several occasions, eager to find his own Achilles heel, keen to anticipate and mitigate the circumstances which might bring him down.

He was ambitious, yes, that was certain. Fiercely ambitious, to the extent that he would do anything to succeed in his plans. But he didn't have any ghosts in his closet. He wasn't gay and he had no interest in young women, or any women, come to that. He was preoccupied only with his own success and power. One day he hoped to become an MP, so he could scale up his enterprise.

Edward Callow knew what drove him. First, a burning desire to escape the poverty he'd experienced as a child and never have to worry about money ever again. That fired him; it was the fuel which drove his powerful engine. Secondly, he would never again be a victim. As a child and teenager, he'd been bullied mercilessly.

One day, he'd had a realisation; it was the day he discovered leverage. He paid some bigger and stronger idiot to beat up the kid who was bullying him. It was simple; he hired the nut-job from the other school in the town where he lived and got him to sort out the nut-job at his own school.

One shattered arm and a lost eye later, Edward was clear of his problem and the underground hero of any child who'd ever been at the receiving end of the kid's fist. It was his first taste of taking control, and it was intoxicating.

As he looked across at Fred Walker now, he could see that he was doing precisely the same thing: using leverage. Only Fred Walker didn't require violence, he just needed a nudge in the right direction. Fred's weakness had been having an affair and getting caught out with a secret love child. That secret would go a long, long way in the leverage stakes. He'd got his eye on a local-copper-made-good too. His influence would come in handy. And he'd read about a local author who'd just landed himself a film deal and was seeking investment opportunities, preferably in his home town. It was all coming together nicely.

'So, Fred, bearing in mind all those hungry mouths to feed and your wife's undoubted pride in how committed you are to your business and your family, I hope you won't mind that I've already pressed the go button on my plan.'

'Will Councillor White come on board? How will you make him? He's dead set against me being awarded the contract.'

Edward smiled. This was his territory. The sooner Fred Walker understood what he brought to the party, the sooner they could all get on and enjoy the undoubted fruits that would soon be borne by their little consortium.

'Ah, here's my man now,' he said, looking up to see Bruce Craven walking into the bar. 'Fred, this is Bruce Craven, an associate of mine who's been doing some work for me during the past month or so. Bruce, this is Fred

Walker. When are you due back at the holiday camp, Bruce? Have you time to join us for a drink?'

'Yeah, I'm good for another half-hour,' Bruce replied. 'Mine's a pint,' he shouted across to the man at the bar.

'I'll pay for a taxi back to Middleton Tower,' Edward told him. 'No need to bother with the buses.'

Bruce's pint arrived, and he downed a third of it straight away. Edward clocked that; he needed Bruce to be in control, not careless through over-consumption of alcohol.

'So, how did it go?' Edward asked as Bruce placed his glass back on the table. 'Was Councillor White up for negotiation?'

Bruce's face turned into a confident smirk. This was exactly what Edward liked about him: Bruce was something he could never be. This man, discovered by accident at The Battery pub four weeks earlier, was like the bully that Edward had hired as a child to do his dirty work. Edward's hands were clean, the payments were in cash, and Bruce was cheap too; he had no idea of the value of his services.

'Let's put it this way: Councillor White is now very excited about the prospect of the contract being awarded to Walker Homes and Construction. Next time you see him, you must pass on your best wishes to him for his wife's health. She had a fall and has broken her wrist. She's in a bad way.'

CHAPTER SEVEN

Morecambe - Present Day

'We have to go to the hospital now!' Will insisted, drained and struggling to keep up with the pace of events. It seemed that everywhere he and Charlotte turned, someone was lurking in the shadows.

His head was still throbbing. He didn't know if it was the earlier blow, or just the sheer volume of information that he was processing.

'How will we get there?' Rex asked. 'I'm public enemy number one at the moment. You might want to go on your own. It could be safer.'

Will stopped for a moment to think it through.

'You're right,' he replied. 'You need to keep a low profile. Are you all right hiding in that boarded-up shop? I've got a fiver in my pocket. It won't even buy me a taxi to Lancaster; you're welcome to take it.'

'Help yourself to whatever's in the fridge,' Vern suggested. 'There's milk in there and a couple of snack bars.

You're welcome to have whatever you want. I'm so grateful to you for finding me. I could have been lying there until at least Monday morning.'

Will had forgotten about Vern. He was an old man, and he'd had a shock. They couldn't just leave him.

'Oh, by the way, those crooks didn't get everything.' Vern smiled. 'Take a look in that old recorder over there.'

Will followed his eyes and walked through to the shop. There was an old and grubby video recorder sitting on the counter.

'Go on, open it up,' Vern said.

Will pressed the button. An unlabelled, black videotape popped out.

'Take it,' Vern said. 'Those bastards didn't get all your tapes. I may be an old bugger, but I'm not stupid. If they'd go to those lengths to get hold of the videos, I figured there must be something on them that somebody doesn't want to be seen. Help yourself. I'd been running that through on fast forward to make sure it copied properly.'

'You realise I'm a fugitive?' Rex asked. 'When the police get here, you're welcome to report me, but I'd rather you didn't. I'll hand myself in once we get ahead of this thing. I'm on the run from some powerful men. Our local MP is one of them...'

'That Callow fellow?' Vern said. 'Never liked him. You can see it in his eyes. His soul is empty. I won't say a thing. It comes to something when the guys who are supposed to be the baddies come and help a frail old man and the so-called goodies are the ones that beat him up in the first place. Besides, I saw what was on those videos. I'm not sure what's going on, but I've got a feeling about them, and it's not a good one.'

Will handed Rex the tape.

'Take this and stay hidden at the boarded-up shop. Don't move from there; keep the video safe at all costs. If they don't know we've got it, we're slightly ahead of them. I'm heading for the infirmary to check on Olli and Charlotte. I'll keep that fiver if you've got enough food, Rex. I can get a taxi back to the guest house then pick up the car from there.'

Rex helped himself to a plastic bag from the side of the counter and wrapped up the videocassette. He shook Will's hand.

'I realise you've no reason to trust me,' he began, 'but believe me, these men are dangerous. Make sure your family are safe and find out where your daughter is, then we need to move together to beat them. If we surface too early, they'll get to us. Find your daughter, Will, then we strike. I spent a lot of years in prison for that bastard, Callow. I want to see him spend the rest of his sorry life in jail.'

Rex checked on Vern, then left the shop, having loaded up with snacks from the fridge. Will used the shop phone and dialled 999. He gave them the address details from Vern and checked he was okay.

'You did well here tonight, Vern. Take care. The ambulance will be here soon.'

Will walked out into the street, making sure to leave the lights on so the ambulance crew would know where to go. They were making the medical teams work overtime that night, that was for sure. As he walked up the road, heading towards the sea front, a taxi drove by. He put out his hand, and the taxi pulled over.

'I'm on my way to Hest Bank,' said the driver. 'Where are you headed, mate?'

'Near the town hall, on the front; it's on your way.'

'Hop in,' the taxi driver said.

Will was relieved; with only a fiver in his pocket, his travel options were limited. This would get him home in the least amount of time. Deciding to call DCI Summers, he fumbled in his pocket for his phone. The battery was almost wiped out, and he'd missed a call from Nigel Davies. Nigel was in Lancaster. Will decided he must have news, so called him first.

'Nigel, it's Will. What news?'

'Charlotte and Olli have been admitted to hospital, you'll be pleased to know.'

'Have you seen them?' Will asked. 'Are they safe?'

'Yes, they're safe. Why? Is something bothering you?'

'Maybe. Are there any cops around?'

'Yes, DCI Summers has been speaking to your wife, and they've posted a copper at the entrance to Olli's ward so they can speak to him as soon as he comes round.'

Will let out a sigh. At last, some good news.

'Anything about your daughter?' Nigel asked.

'No, I'm just about to check at the guest house, then I'm coming over to the infirmary. I'm praying Lucia will be home after what I just heard, and we can get this whole sorry episode finished. I'm really scared, I think she may be in terrible danger. Where are you now? Can you get a message to Charlotte?'

'I'm not at the infirmary,' Nigel replied. 'I'm at the private unit where Edward Callow has been admitted. But the wily bugger's checking out any time now.'

'What happened to him? Was it an attempt on his life?'

'He wants everybody to think that,' Nigel said, the cynicism dripping from his voice. 'If you ask me, it was a scam. He got his private physician to say he'd had a mild heart attack brought on by threats from whoever it was who killed

Fred Walker. He's lucky to be alive; apparently they left him for dead in his car.'

'Don't tell me, he didn't get a proper look at them?'

'Of course, he didn't,' Nigel continued. 'And I've never seen a man look so healthy after a supposed heart attack. The other reporters are lapping up the story, but I'm having none of it. That man is in this up to his ears if you ask me.'

'That's four pounds mate,' the taxi driver said.

Will had been so engrossed in the call that he'd barely noticed where they were.

'Keep the change,' he replied, handing over the five-pound note. He got out of the vehicle and continued his call.

'Where's Edward Callow now?' Will asked. As he spoke, his phone beeped once.

'You won't believe it if I tell you,' came Nigel's voice. 'He's just been wheeled out to a waiting car, looking every inch the invalid. He even has a blanket over his knees. That picture will be in the Sunday papers tomorrow. If I were a betting man, I'd say Edward Callow just created his perfect cover story for the police. They'll be wondering why he's not dead yet, just like all his pals. Now he can claim they came for him and he was saved by his dodgy heart. He's a clever man, this one. We need to be careful near him.'

Will was at the front door of the guest house now. He fumbled for his key. They always locked it from midnight.

'I'm heading over to Lancaster now,' Will said, inserting the key and turning it in the lock. He could see there was still activity in the lounge. The lights were still on in there and in the kitchen.

'Will I catch you there?' he asked.

'Not sure,' said Nigel. 'It's been a long day, so I'll call it a night here and see how the land lies tomorrow. I'll keep my phone on. Call me if you hear anything about your daughter; it doesn't matter what—'

'Shit!' Will cursed. His phone vibrated and shut down. He was out of battery, and Charlotte still had his charging pack. He went into the hall, checked the kitchen, then walked into the lounge. George and Isla were there, with a sleepy Una lying on the floor at their feet. The dog's ears pricked up as soon as Will walked into the lounge. She sprang to her feet, wagging her tail enthusiastically.

'Hello, Una,' Will said, stroking her back. 'Any sign of Lucia?' he asked. He could see what the answer was from the look on their faces.

'Sorry, Will. No calls, no knocks at the door. Have the police said anything?'

'No, I'm worried out of my mind. That girl's got some explaining to do when we find her. I've been patient up to now, but I'm beginning to agree with Charlotte; she needs a firm hand.'

'And Charlotte and Olli?' George asked.

He could see how concerned George was; he'd always had a soft spot for Charlotte, ever since their days at the campsite.

'In hospital and safe,' Will said.

'I've spoken to Isla about you-know-what,' George began.

'You mean your cancer?' Isla interrupted. 'Call it what it is, George. It's cancer, and you're going to beat it.'

George looked up at Will. They'd already discussed that matter. He had no intention of arguing with Isla, who would be in desperate need of a few straws to clutch at if she'd just heard the news. Will could hear the front door being unlocked, and his heart skipped for a moment, praying it might be Lucia. He walked out to the hall to see if it was her.

'Oh, hello, you're still up. You keep long hours.'

It was Daisy Bowker, dressed like she'd been out.

'How are the family, Will? Any news?'

'He shook his head. Charlotte and Olli are fine, but there's still no news of Lucia.'

'I'm sure she'll turn up. Teenagers can be devils. And it's a Saturday night, too. She'll be out enjoying herself without a care in the world.'

'Hopefully,' Will said, not at all reassured by her words.

'Have you been anywhere nice?'

It was an automatic question, one which they always asked guests when they returned late at night.

'Well, you'll never guess who I met tonight. What a wealth of information she had about the Sandy Beaches Holiday Camp. And she says she knows you and Charlotte well. In fact, you were with her only last night.'

Will knew who Daisy was talking about before the name came out of her mouth. It was Abi Smithson. Of course it was; it was only a matter of time before somebody would tell her all about Abi.

CHAPTER EIGHT

Morecambe - Present Day

Charlotte had been right to warn him about Daisy Bowker. Here she was making connections on her own, talking to the locals, getting closer to Bruce all the time. The way Will felt, he was ready to give it all up, tell the truth, and just take whatever was coming their way. How bad could it be, after what had just happened to Olli?

Yet Abi had a secret too, one which she would not wish to reveal; she'd once confided in him that Bruce had fathered her child after a brief fling three years before he and Charlotte worked at the holiday camp. But would Abi see Daisy's questioning as a good thing? Probably not; she thought Bruce was still alive, since she knew nothing of George's final revelation that Jenna had killed him and that he was still buried underneath the concrete base of the pool.

So Daisy's appearance would be equally unwelcome to Abi. If she believed Bruce to be alive, she'd never reveal that he was the father, because it might bring him back into her life. She was as pleased as everybody else to see the back of him. Abi must have lied to Daisy, just as he and Charlotte had. That was good. It would steer her away from what really happened.

'Oh yes, we know Abi. She's a great singer,' Will said, thinking of the blandest, most non-committal thing he could say.

'She thinks the world of you, credits you with Simon Cowell-like powers. Were you really responsible for her singing career?'

'I think that's a bit generous,' Will replied. 'I just gave her a little push to use her considerable talents. She needed more confidence, that's all. Look, I have to get to the hospital to see if they'll let me in to see Charlotte and Olli. I need to excuse myself, I'm afraid.'

'Can I come?' Daisy asked. 'I'm wide awake and buzzing after my conversation with Abi, and I wouldn't mind talking about it in the car. Besides, I've grown rather fond of that wife of yours. We had a lovely chat on our way to parkrun this morning.'

Will wasn't sure how to answer, but he figured that a no would just make Daisy even more suspicious. She seemed less confrontational about her half-brother's whereabouts since she'd chatted to Abi, so it made sense to catch up with what she'd discovered and see if she was any further forward.

'Sure,' he said. 'George and Isla, I'm heading to Lancaster. My phone is dead, so if Lucia turns up or gets in contact, please call Charlotte or get a message through to the infirmary. Thanks for helping out tonight; we appreciate it.'

'Send our love to Charlotte and Olli,' Isla said, 'And of course we'll alert you and the police if we hear anything from Lucia. Be safe. You still look terrible after your run-in earlier this evening. Are you sure you're okay to drive?'

Will was anything but certain about driving, but he decided to risk it anyway. Besides, if he did have a prang, he was restricted to 30 mph most of the way to Lancaster, so he wouldn't come to any harm, and the roads were quieter now.

He ran up the stairs to check Lucia's bedroom and the rest of the family's living quarters before leaving, needing to be certain that Lucia wasn't there. She wasn't. Will wanted to scream in frustration. He was seriously considering in confiding in DCI Summers if she was still at the hospital; it was too much for him. And he just wanted it all to be over.

As he and Daisy headed out of Morecambe towards Lancaster, they exchanged pleasantries about the resort and local area. Then Daisy dropped the inevitable bombshell.

'So you and Charlotte did know Bruce well, it seems? And by all accounts, you and Abi were close friends.'

'It was a long time ago,' Will answered, struggling more than usual to pick things out under the street lamps as he drove. He hadn't managed to focus properly since he'd been attacked. He would make sure Charlotte and Olli were taken care of, then get himself checked out at A&E.

'I can't remember it all now. It's so long ago. Thirty-five years ago, to be exact. I can hardly remember what happened five minutes ago, let alone three decades previously.'

Daisy laughed.

'I know that feeling,' she agreed. 'Why do I sense that Bruce wasn't well-liked? There's no warmth there when people refer to him. I'd like to think I would make an impression on the people I worked with.'

Will thought back to the time when Bruce had held his

hand beneath the spout of the tea urn and scalded his skin, and when he'd hijacked him and Charlotte as they got off the late bus after their first day in Morecambe. Then there was the night when Bruce attacked Charlotte on the beach, and they both thought they'd killed him.

Daisy was right. Now he thought about it, there never seemed to be much laughter around Bruce Craven. He was intense and quiet, not a big talker. Will burned with jealousy and hatred whenever he thought of Charlotte with that man. It had only been a short-lived relationship, and he knew that Charlotte despised Bruce when she realised what he really was. But Will struggled with knowing that his wife had been intimate with Bruce, even though it was so long ago; he was pleased the man was dead.

'As Charlotte and I said, there were so many people working at the camp. We can barely remember most of them. Abi was in the room opposite me. We used to socialise as a group, me, Charlotte, Abi, Sally, her boyfriend...'

Jenna's name was on the tip of his tongue.

'And who's this girl, Jenna?' Daisy asked.

Damn. Abi had mentioned Jenna. Why wouldn't she? Jenna played no important part in Abi's story. But Jenna could blow the whole thing wide open, especially about their relationships with Bruce. And she could do that without revealing what she did to him.

'Oh yes, and her too. I'm not sure what happened to her.'

'Abi reckoned Charlotte used to meet her for coffee when you returned to Morecambe. She said she's in prison now.'

Will had been caught in a lie.

'Oh, Jenna,' he replied. 'I thought you said Jenny. She

was somebody else who worked at the camp, I misheard you, sorry.'

He felt his face burning and thanked his luck that the lighting was poor.

'We're here now,' he said, pulling into the car park for the infirmary. 'I'm sorry to ask, but do you have some coins for the parking? I didn't bring any with me. I assume they still charge at this time of night. I'm surprised they don't double down and extract a pint of blood from us too, while they're at it.'

There was plenty of parking at that time of night, but because there were barriers in place, they decided not to risk it and bought a ticket before walking

over to the main hospital complex.

'I haven't a clue where I'm going,' Will said, stopping on the pavement and looking for the nearest blue sign. He found one and studied the options.

'Any ideas where to start?' he asked. 'Despite the events of this evening, I haven't spent all that much time in hospitals.'

'Let's ask in A&E,' Daisy suggested. 'At least they'll be able to point us in the right direction. It's a Saturday night. It's bound to be a party in there.'

They stepped into A&E and surveyed the waiting area. It wasn't bad, bearing in mind it must have been the shift the staff dreaded most.

'I'll find a nurse or a doctor,' Daisy said. 'See if you can figure out where we're heading from the cluster of signs by that door.'

It seemed like a good enough plan. Will had decided he would check himself into here before he drove back to Morecambe. He was sure he was displaying the signs of a concussion that he'd read about earlier, and was beginning to worry.

As he was studying the signs up ahead, two men walked by. He sensed them before he saw them; they had a presence that you could almost reach out and touch. Then his ear was drawn by the rasping sound of a man's voice. He glanced at them as they passed by, confidently heading for the doorway, taking a left turn like they had every right to be there. The guy with the grating voice was probably ill; maybe he had throat cancer. Or was it a coincidence?

Something made Will turn as the electronic sliding doors behind him swished open. Walking into A&E was the man with the purple Mohican, styled into the shape of a dragon.

CHAPTER NINE

Morecambe - 1984

'I hope you'll understand why I have to make this enquiry, Mr Callow. We have to take these allegations seriously.'

Edward sat opposite the detective constable in the meeting room he'd booked at the Town Hall, squirming with embarrassment at being questioned in his workplace.

He could barely contain his fury at Bruce Craven. The man was an imbecile. He might have an excellent capacity for calm violence, but he was lacking in the brains department. After working for them for only five weeks, he'd already brought trouble to Edward's door.

'Yes, I understand,' Edward replied, his voice cautious. 'I'd expect nothing less... sorry, what did you say your name was again?'

'DC Harvey Turnbull. Soon to be DCI actually.'

'Congratulations,' Edward replied. 'So tell me, what are Councillor White's allegations and why do you believe that it's anything to do with me?'

'Councillor White alleges that this man...' he referred to his notes. 'Bruce Craven. This chap allegedly confronted the Councillor and his wife in their garden. We have a witness, one of the neighbours who saw what was going on. The Councillor says that you have been exerting great pressure on him to withdraw his objections to your tender for the new school. So, as you can see, I have to follow this up, even though I suspect it's just paranoia on White's part. I'm sure you understand we still have to go through the formal processes.'

Edward could see his dreams going up in smoke. He'd got everything planned out, but Fred Walker had to deliver this high profile local project to show that he was capable of a huge infrastructure contract. From that point, they'd be ready to take on the world. White was a well-known local moaner, but Edward had called it wrong. He'd thought a single threat to the man's wife would do the job and intimidate him. He'd underestimated the boring little man.

'This is an interesting time for you and Fred Walker,' Turnbull continued, changing the subject. 'That school project must be worth a fair few bob. You won't need to work in the Town Hall much longer if you pull that one off.'

Edward studied Turnbull's face. He'd never met the man before, but he appeared to be a straight dealer. It was unusual for a DC to call on such a trivial matter too. Was he reaching out to Edward? Turnbull had referred to the councillor's paranoia, that seemed a little indiscreet for a public servant. He decided to test it.

'Yes, it's a challenge,' Edward replied. 'To tell you the truth, it's more challenging than I thought it would be. I'm in the market for new partners. People who could advise me on certain issues of which I have little knowledge.'

DC Turnbull stood up from the small table that separated them and walked over to the door. It hadn't been closed properly, so he turned the handle and made sure it was properly shut. He walked slowly back to his chair and sat down once again.

'I'm guessing security will be one of those issues that's weighing on your mind?' Turnbull asked.

Edward was certain this man was reaching out. Was he a crooked cop? A plant within the local police force could be useful.

'Yes, we'll need to look at security issues. Take this Craven fellow, for instance. Of course, I've never heard of the man, but if somebody did send him to intimidate the councillor, you'd need a person who was much more reliable than that. Someone who could get the job done without attracting any attention.'

Turnbull nodded. Edward might have been mistaken, but he thought he saw a flicker in his eyes, like a newly ignited flame.

'I've just been dealing with a guy who should be doing work like that. He's a chap called Bob Moseley, a local chap, born and bred in Morecambe. He knows everyone and everybody. A real tough nut, he is. He talks like he just swallowed a bucketful of gravel. Got stabbed in the throat as a young man, apparently, and swore it would never happen to him again. Violent bugger, he is, but he knows how to stay out of sight of the law. He was clean as a whistle when I looked into him. Now that's the type of man you need, not a blundering idiot like this Craven man.'

'I expect that whoever did send Craven will want him taken care of now. A loose cannon like him can't be left unattended after all.'

'Just what I was thinking.' Turnbull smiled. 'You'd need a man just like Moseley.'

Edward had a fish nibbling on the end of the line. It was time to reel him in.

'I expect your wife will be delighted that you've got this promotion? Do you have a family?'

'Yes, I've got kids who are eating me out of house and home. I had to take the promotion because we've lost my wife's salary. You know what it's like, loads more pressure at work and little in return. What can you do? Lots of coppers have second jobs, just to make ends meet. I'm thinking of branching out myself.'

'Have you ever considered getting involved in a project like the rebuilding of the secondary school, DC Turnbull? May I call you Harvey?'

'I wouldn't have a clue where to begin,' Turnbull replied. 'My skills lie elsewhere.'

'As a local police officer, you must know everything and everybody. I'll bet there are also a fair few secrets running about this town, too? I'm sure you could tell some stories.'

'I absolutely could!' Turnbull smiled. 'Take Councillor White, for instance...'

Turnbull paused. Edward noted it; the detective was figuring out if he had the guts to take the next leap. Fortunately, he did.

'White has a previous police record for exposing himself to women in public parks, did you know that? He moved to Morecambe from a place near London. He was let off with a caution, but nobody up here knows about it. Imagine what a man like Bob Moseley could do with that information, delivered with a nice topping of menace. People like this Bruce Craven fellow are lightweights by comparison. They're all muscle and no strategy.'

The cogs in Edward's mind were whirring like a machine on speed. If this was a leap of faith for DC Turnbull, it was supping with the devil for Edward. He could see how a contact like Turnbull would be useful. That information alone about Councillor White was all he needed for the pain in the arse moaner to withdraw his objections to the tender being awarded to Fred. It was as simple as that; it seemed that everybody had skeletons in their closet if you only dug deep enough.

'I'll bet you could use a few extra shifts, with a growing family. There's a large amount of profit to be taken from this deal if it goes through. We'll be re-investing a lot of it in plant and equipment, but we'll be skimming off substantial amounts to remunerate the key partners. We could do with a man like you on the team, in an advisory capacity. You're well-connected, and you've got great experience in security matters. What would it take to get you on board?'

This question seemed to throw Turnbull. Like Edward, his salary would be restricted to pay scales and annual capped increases. His imagination would be limited. Edward decided to deploy a trick he'd seen on the TV. He reached across to a grab a small notepad that had been left on the table in the meeting room and pulled a pen out of his shirt pocket. Swiftly, he ran through the calculations in his head.

As a DCI, Turnbull would be earning more than Edward was. He tried to place himself in Turnbull's shoes. If the deal fell through, he'd end up with one mighty pissed-off police officer on his case. His offer had to be attractive enough to make sure Turnbull sorted Councillor Edwards for good. He needed that man—that pervert—to stop opposing Fred Walker's bid. If they landed the deal, Edward would never have to worry about his own crappy salary ever again.

Edward shielded the paper with his left arm and wrote

down a cash figure. Without saying a word, he turned the pad so that Turnbull could see it.

The look on Turnbull's face said it all. It was more money than he'd seen in a long time, enough to fan that small ember in his eyes into a hungry flame.

'Yeah, that should just about do it,' Turnbull said. Edward could almost see him running the numbers in his head; an extension, a nice holiday, maybe an upgrade on the car. This would accelerate Turnbull in a way that a move from DC to DCI never could.

Edward turned the paper round and wrote another number on the pad.

'Maybe I didn't make myself clear,' he said, scribbling a second number on the pad. 'That amount is to secure your consultation services on this project. Cash in hand, on delivery of the first payment made through the contract if—when—we win it. The second sum is the bonus you'll get as soon as the tender is awarded. When Councillor White stops playing hardball and decides to support Fred Walker's bid.'

This time Harvey Turnbull was unable to contain himself when Edward turned the pad round. Edward would make this payment from his personal savings. It would be worth it to get White on side at last and get the tender awarded in their favour.

'Fuck me!' Turnbull said, unable to contain himself.

'I take it we're in business together?' Edward asked.

'We certainly are,' came the reply.

DC Turnbull got out of his seat, shook Edward's hand and walked towards the door.

'Oh, DC Turnbull,' Edward said. 'One more thing before you go.'

Turnbull turned to face him.

'If I were the man who'd employed Bruce Craven to make such a mess of that job with Councillor White, I'd want him removed and out of harm's way as soon as possible, wouldn't you?'

'I agree with you totally,' Turnbull replied. 'I wouldn't want a prick like that bad-mouthing you to his drinking pals. Idiots like him get what's coming to them.'

CHAPTER TEN

Morecambe - Present Day

Will knew he'd made a mistake the moment he did it.

'Hey, I need a word with you! Where's my daughter?'

The man with the purple Mohican took one look at him and bolted for the door. Will had no intention of letting him go. He was the closest link he had to Lucia. As the man disappeared through the sliding doors of A&E, he heard Daisy calling after him.

'Will? What on earth are you—?'

He didn't wait to explain. As he followed the man through the doors, he cursed himself for not thinking more clearly. He'd acted on gut instinct. There were police officers in the building, so why the hell hadn't he just let DCI Summers or one of her colleagues know that this man was involved in Lucia's disappearance? He could have trailed behind all three men and just followed them. What a dick-head he was.

Already Will was out of breath. The man with the

Mohican had bolted through the doors, avoiding the car park and heading away from the hospital. Although he was still struggling with his sight, Will could tell that he was trying to phone his mates to warn them. He had to catch this man and find out where Lucia was. Even as he ran, his head pounding, his eyesight blurred and his legs aching, Will knew that he had to leave the man with the grating voice and his pal to DCI Summers and her colleagues. If this man got away, they might lose their connection to Lucia.

Will was struggling for breath now, but so was his prey. Up ahead, he could see the man stop at the junction at the end of the road. He was catching his breath, as if confident that he had enough of a lead on Will to spare a few seconds.

'I only want to talk to you!' Will shouted through his panting. It was an embarrassing thing to say, but he didn't know how long he could keep up this chase, and he couldn't face the agony of losing this man in the darkness.

The man with the Mohican gave him the finger and started to run again. Will followed, cursing him and scolding himself for getting so out of shape. He watched as his target crossed the road, darting into a side street to take cover. Will trained his eyes on the moving figure ahead, not daring to lose him for a second.

Across the road was a medical centre with a car park behind it. Will's pounding heart was outdone only by the relentless thumping in his head. He scanned the entrance to the medical centre, making sure his quarry wasn't hiding in the recess there. He must have moved round into the car park. There were only two cars there. Will guessed they belonged to nearby residents who were taking advantage of a bit of free off-street parking. He scanned below the cars, looking for any movement between the chassis and the asphalt. For the first time, it struck him that he was vulnerable to assault. He would be no match if the man turned aggressive. Why hadn't he considered that before giving chase?

The car park was quiet. There was foliage there, but nothing too substantial. There must be something he could use if the man sprang out at him and attacked. Damn his phone for running out of battery.

Near the entrance to the car park, a small tree had had one of its smaller branches broken off, no doubt by kids or passing vandals. It would make a lamentable weapon, but it might at least give him something with which to protect himself. The branch was only half-broken off the tree, so he had to twist and pull it to free it. As he did so, he continued to monitor the car park for signs of movement. He snapped off several smaller twigs and held the branch in his hand. It was heavy enough to deter someone. It would have to do.

There was movement up ahead, fast footsteps running across the asphalt. The man with the Mohican had darted out from behind a car and was now making his way towards the far end of the car park. Will followed him, grateful for the few minutes he'd had to catch his breath. He cursed as he watched his target leap over a single wooden fence panel which separated the surgery grounds from the main road outside. It was a six-foot panel, but the man made light of it, running up to it at speed and vaulting over the top. Will knew how that would play out when it was his turn.

If he lost this man now, he'd lose his daughter; failure was not an option, despite the odds being against him. Will ran up to the fence panel and jumped up at it. There was no way he could pull himself over it. But he spotted it was worn and in need of a paint, the type of flimsy DIY store panel which easily blew down in the wind.

'Fuck it!' he said aloud and ran at the panel, his shoulder braced for impact. He heard a snap as the rotted wooden post holding it in place broke off. Two more pushes and he was through, albeit in a much less athletic manner than the person he was pursuing.

Will looked up and down the road. He thought he'd lost his prey, then caught sight of his rear end darting inside the ornate gate of a private school. He'd seen the youngsters walking about Lancaster in their smart uniforms, but he'd never been inside the gates. If it was a private school, it would likely be old-fashioned and set in extensive grounds. The apocalyptic landscape of a local secondary school would have been preferable. There would have been fewer places to hide.

Will waited by the ornate gate, an imposing stone structure with two arches, one at either side of the driveway. Each arch was supported by a heavy, stone pillar capped with a conical structure and topped with hand-carved crosses. Between two of the main pillars was a substantial yet decorative wrought-iron gate. The gates were open, presumably to allow access to the gatehouse, but ahead of them, the drive was closed, protected by a low, more functional modern barrier.

Caught off guard, Will became aware of a movement to his side. He tensed his body, trying to work out what was happening. Before he'd had time to brace himself, something struck him hard on the head. As a child, Will had laughed at comics which showed cartoon characters whose heads were surrounded by stars or cheeping birds whenever they were struck on the head. But that was exactly what he experienced.

His mind went blank for a second, like a PC stuttering to load its operating system. Will dropped to his knees, a sick feeling deep in his stomach, his mind swirling and his vision seriously impaired. He sensed his attacker moving at his side. Will was still holding his branch. He brandished it in as threatening a manner as he could manage, but the man with the Mohican only laughed at him. Will could see the rounded stone that had been thrown at him, lying just to the side of one of the wrought-iron gates.

'You silly bugger!' the man scoffed. 'Your wife runs a lot faster than you do. It's time you started eating a lot less, old man.'

This was the gloating idiot who'd been speaking to Lucia. He was in spitting distance now. Will had to hang on; he mustn't let him go. He fought with his clouded mind, struggling to get a grip on his surroundings and what was going on around him.

'You should have backed off,' the man continued. 'That wife of yours is in it up to her neck. My mates are just about to sort out her and your son. As for your daughter, she's a nice-looking young woman; I fancy her myself. She's very trusting too, stupid fool.'

Will spotted something glinting. It had just caught a street light. He had a knife. This disgusting man was armed.

'Just so you know, before I cut your throat, your daughter gets to live. The trouble is, she'll soon wish she was dead. And when I see her next, I'll tell her how useless her old man was. That he was so out of shape, he couldn't even keep up with me.'

This was it. If Will couldn't come up with an idea in the next few seconds, it was over. The man was leaning against the gate, his left hand resting on one of the ornate curls in the ironwork. By his feet was the heavy stone that he'd thrown at Will. He had the branch too. Will fought through the fog of his thoughts and came up with a plan, his final chance. He would have to be quick.

'Anyway old man, there's a hot teenage girl who needs a little attention, I can't keep her waiting all...'

Will rose to his feet and charged at him. The knife was thrust out in self-defence, but Will had reckoned on that, defending himself with the branch in his hand. His opponent had been caught out, thinking he had Will at his mercy.

Pushing the blade away with the branch so that it fell to the ground, Will picked up the stone and pushed his assailant into the wrought-iron gate. As he put out his hand to steady himself, Will spotted an opportunity that he hadn't expected. The man's hand was resting on top of one of the iron spikes that formed part of the gate's design, thrust out as he'd tried to steady himself. Will raised the stone and hammered it on the top of his hand, impaling him on the tapered point.

'Jesus Christ!' the man cried.

The man with the Mohican swore again, then passed out with the pain, his hand impaled securely on the iron spike. He wouldn't be able to remove it without tearing his flesh.

'Fuck you, fuck you!' Will screamed, a massive surge of fear and adrenaline coursing through his body. He took the man's phone, made sure that he was securely impaled on the gate, kicked away the knife, then began to run back to the hospital. There were two more of these thugs to deal with before he would allow himself to drop.

CHAPTER ELEVEN

Morecambe - Present Day

Will fought to stay conscious, his head swirling as if in a black hole, wanting to vomit at the realisation of what he'd just done to that man. The thought of the iron spike tearing through the sinews of his hand made him shudder; how had he done such a terrible thing? But he'd had no choice, if he was to survive and find Lucia; at least the thug wasn't going anywhere while he was pinned on that gate.

Will headed for the hospital. He'd alert the police, get the place searched, and make sure Olli and Charlotte were safe. Now the guy with the Mohican was captured, he'd lead them to Lucia, and they could rescue her from whatever terrible thing they'd planned for her.

Will began to sob at what he'd done to his family, as he dragged himself back towards the entrance of the A&E building. He'd taken the children out of school, relocated them to Morecambe almost on a whim and wrecked their lives in the process. What the hell had he been thinking?

It was a crazy move, all because the guest house was going for a song and he'd seen a way out of their financial dilemma and a possible path through Charlotte's fragile mental health. It all came back to that bastard Bruce Craven. He was long dead, but his evil influence was reaching from beyond the grave in an attempt to drag them all to burn in hell with him. He would never forgive himself if anything happened to Lucia.

Will heard a phone ringing. It was the device he'd taken from the man with the purple hair. He answered.

'Tyler? Where are you?'

A gritty, coarse voice came over the speaker.

'Your man is fucked. And now I'm coming for you.'

Will couldn't believe those words were coming out of his mouth. But he wanted them to know he meant business.

'Mr Grayson, I assume? Where are you now, in Lancaster? Better move quickly, we're just about to suffocate your wife with her hospital pillow. Same for your son, then we'll get to work on your daughter. Goodbye, Mr Grayson. Just think, that interfering bitch of a wife of yours will be struggling to take her final breath any moment now.'

The call was ended. Will was poised to ring the police, but they were there already, in the hospital. It would take him longer to get hold of them than it would to get the hospital reception to alert them. He thought of calling DCI Summers, but without his own phone fully charged, he didn't have her number. Will started to run again. He had to get to her.

Although his head was aching and his limbs were stiff, Will pressed on, focusing on the narrow strip of red on the signage ahead of him, indicating the location of the A&E department. His lungs were on fire with the pain of exertion, but he made it to the sliding doors, bursting into the reception area.

A nurse looked up as he entered and grimaced at his appearance. Will touched his head and his hand came away wet, with blood no doubt. He hated to think what he looked like now, but at least he was in the right place. Once he'd made sure Charlotte and Olli were safe, he'd direct them to the man who was impaled on the gate, then he could rest. Only then would he close his eyes and let the pounding in his head come to an end.

'I need the police... where are the police?'

He couldn't form his words properly. The nurse looked at him, her attitude changing; she thought he was drunk.

'Go and take a seat, we'll be with you as soon as we can,' she said.

'I'm not... I'm not drunk,' he said. He couldn't get his mouth to work. He'd read about people having strokes. Surely that wasn't happening to him? Not a stroke, not now.

'Please, sir, take a seat. If you need to have a drink of water to sober yourself up, there's a water machine over there.'

'But I'm not... I'm not...'

Will gave up. She was losing patience with him. He looked towards the reception desk. The hospital was huge, and he hadn't a clue where Charlotte and Olli would be. The man with the gravelly voice had gone through the door at the other end of A&E. He and his companion had seemed to know where they were heading. He would follow their lead.

Even in his confused state of mind, Will knew he'd made the wrong call in chasing Tyler; it had been a distraction. But at least the police would soon have him in custody.

Getting him off that spike would be a lot harder than pushing him onto it had been.

As Will made his way through the corridors of the hospital, the few people still around watched him warily, stepping out of his way as he approached them. He could only guess what he looked like. What the hell was he doing, rushing about the hospital with no plan? He had no idea where Charlotte was. He could be wandering about all night.

There was a workstation up ahead with a reception desk where a nurse was working, with the lights dimmed around her. She was tapping a keyboard. Will approached in as calm a way as he could manage. The nurse sensed his presence before he got there.

'Can you... please help me...?' he slurred. She was wary of him. He watched as her hand moved to the receiver on her phone, ready to summon security, no doubt.

'Please, don't call security. My wife and son are here; they were... they were brought here earlier. I must see them. I'm not drunk... I'm...'

The nurse's hand moved from the receiver back to her keyboard.

'Let me check,' she said. 'If you're wasting my time, I'll call security and ask for you to be escorted out of the building.'

'Charlotte Grayson and Oliver Grayson. They were ad... ad... admitted this evening.'

Why couldn't he form his words? What was happening to him?

The nurse keyed in the information and checked her screens then looked up at Will.

'And you are?'

'I'm Will, Will Grayson. Charlotte's husband.'

'I see you're noted as next of kin. Look, I'll send you up there, but you'll have to ask the duty team if it's all right for you to visit at this time of night. What happened to you? You look like you need to be in here with the rest of your family.'

Will didn't answer. He just wanted to find Charlotte and Olli.

'They're in separate wards, I'm afraid,' the nurse said, copying the information from the screen. She handed him a small sheet of paper.

'Your wife is closest,' she said. 'Head back up that corridor and turn left. And remember, it's outside visiting hours. They may turn you away when you get there.'

'Thank you, thank you,' Will said. He felt drunk, even though there was no way he could be. If he could just get to Charlotte and Olli...

As Will walked at speed up and down the long, echoing corridors, following the contradictory signage on the walls and moving up one level in the elevator, he spotted the ward he'd been seeking. He walked up to the doubled wooden doors where the name of the ward was written on blue signage. It was protected by an electronic lock, with a door buzzer and camera surveillance. As he pressed the buzzer to get the nursing staff's attention, he prayed that the men hadn't got to Charlotte yet.

CHAPTER TWELVE

Morecambe - 1984

Edward Callow could hardly contain himself. Barry McMillan was the first millionaire he'd ever sat down with for coffee. Sure, he'd been in rooms with millionaires, but he was always playing the role of *miscellaneous person* at times like that, just a planning department suit who facilitated and rubber-stamped the land and property deals that made other people millions. Barry had landed a film franchise deal in Hollywood, and even if the money wasn't in his bank account, it would surely be heading there soon.

That wasn't the only matter pleasing him on that Thursday afternoon; it was Mason Jones who'd sent Barry his way. Mason's primary role had been as an insider and influencer, as the lucrative tender for the new school passed through its tedious journey to a final decision. Sending Barry over with a view to discussing potential investment opportunities had been a brainwave on Mason's part.

Maybe the youthful enthusiasm of his students was rubbing off on him.

The summer season was nearing its end. The Bruce Craven issue was about to be resolved, according to Harvey Turnbull, and they'd find out who was getting the school contract in the first weeks of September. The first turf was to be cut in October. Edward couldn't wait. And now, here was a man bearing gifts.

Edward took an immediate liking to Barry McMillan as he bounded into the café at Dazzle Amusement Arcades. It was an odd place to meet for a business discussion, but Barry part-owned this place. Edward thought he was probably keen to show that he already had skin in the game with his property investments.

Although he'd lived in the resort for several years, Edward had not frequented seaside arcades since he was a young man. It never ceased to amaze him how hordes of visitors would swarm around the machines, bags of loose change in their hand, pouring their hard-earned cash into the slots with little by way of financial return.

Edward's mantra was to place his money in income-producing assets. The time would come when he could waste money and indulge himself, but as a council officer on a restricted salary scale, he needed to be prudent. Already that strategy had paid off for him, as his savings had been sufficient to buy the services of an influential member of the local constabulary.

Edward ventured five pounds in the arcades, which he considered an investment. It would give him something to discuss with Barry McMillan when he arrived. He would be flattered that Edward had spent money in his establishment and it would convey approval before they'd even met. These little things counted.

He'd also done a bit of research on Barry McMillan, cashing in swiftly on his investment in Harvey Turnbull. His theory about men in power was borne out by Barry McMillan; he too had the inevitable weakness of a man at the height of his powers.

As Edward flicked 1p pieces into the Penny Falls game, he counted up in his head how much he'd spent and what his return was. So far, he'd let loose 37p into the machine and won back 21p. However, when the pile of pennies crashed down, he experienced a momentary sense of elation, as if he'd somehow won.

That, in turn, encouraged him to place more pennies into the slot. By the time he'd had enough, he was 56p out of pocket, with three crashes of coins as his reward. He wondered what possessed people to pile their money in and resolved that he would never apply the same principles to his own business. If something had become unprofitable - or was creating a burden - it would be cut loose.

Just like Bruce Craven, whose clumsy attempts at intimidating the councillor had been witnessed by a neighbour. That was a mistake which Edward could not forgive, even if its overall impact had been positive. It had brought Harvey Turnbull to him, who in turn made the issue go away.

Edward had decided to remove Bruce from his employment, but just like a game on the penny falls, he'd made Bruce feel like he'd had a win. Edward had paid cash in hand, bought him a beer and sent him home in a taxi. Bruce Craven would understand within the next couple of days that he'd experienced the thrill of the pennies tumbling and the temporary elation of a win. However, he would soon realise that he'd made a big loss by exposing Edward to police scrutiny.

Edward played a few more games in the arcade and was

surprised at how fast he'd burned up his five pounds. 'Income-producing assets,' he mumbled to himself, looking about him and roughly counting the machines. He reckoned there were about a hundred, and he'd wasted five pounds in twenty minutes. If everybody else was burning money at the same rate as he was, Barry McMillan had invested wisely in a great little goldmine.

He looked at his watch. It was just before three o'clock. He ordered a cup of tea for only ten pence and took a plastic seat at one of the picnic-style tables. Barry joined him at precisely three o'clock. For Edward, that was the perfect start; punctuality was a good sign.

Barry McMillan had a positive energy about him, as well he might, bearing in mind his early financial success. Edward had seen him photographed in the papers; he looked just like his formal author shots. They shook hands. Barry ordered a coffee and joined Edward at the table.

'So what do you think?' Barry asked.

'Very clever,' Edward replied. 'This place is a licence to print money. It must be a great investment.'

'Yes, and we sell the cheapest tea and coffee in More-cambe. A simple thing like that—as well as providing clean toilets and baby-change facilities—keeps us busy throughout the quiet season. It's certainly opened my eyes.'

'So what do you own here?' Edward queried. His own aspirations for wealth were fuelled by ambition. He was learning the business of investment and money manage-ment as he went along.

'I'm a part-owner,' Barry answered, sipping his drink and blowing on it to cool it faster. 'I own a fifth. That's one-fifth of the building, one-fifth of the outgoings and one-fifth of the profits. It gives me a good return, but I want to move into something bigger.'

'How big?' Edward queried. He wanted to assess Barry's appetite.

'My business is writing books,' Barry continued, 'But as I make money from those books, I want to invest it in projects that will yield a strong return and grow that income further. I'm in the lucky position of owning two homes outright now; one in Morecambe and one in London. But now this film franchise is going through, I've got more money than I can spend.'

Edward closed his eyes momentarily and tried to imagine what that would feel like. It gave him a rush, the sensation that whatever happened, he could deal with it financially.

'I need bigger investments. I've generated some risk capital, but it's wasting its time in the bank. I need to sweat it harder.'

'So why me?' Edward asked. He already knew the answer.

'Mason Jones tells me you're part of a consortium that's bidding to build the new school. What better place to invest my money than in the place where my own kids will eventually be educated? I love this town, and I owe it so much; I want to keep my money here if I can.'

'You know the contract hasn't been awarded yet?'

'Yes, I understand how these things work. But Mason says he thinks it's going your way after a councillor withdrew his objections. I want in; I can put a substantial amount of money into the deal to make things work.'

Edward already knew he would say yes to Barry McMillan. There was just one thing bothering him, having committed to using Bruce Craven's clumsy services a little too hastily. He was wary of jumping in too fast. His hand reached into the inner pocket of his jacket, pulling out the sheet of paper that Harvey Turnbull had given him. On that sheet of paper was a list of Barry McMillan's minor misdemeanours.

There was nothing too bad in there, but Barry McMillan appeared to have an inclination for risk-taking behaviour. It was all of the middle-class variety: stopped twice and sent on his way for drink-driving, and one incident of alleged kerb-crawling, which was kept quiet on the instructions of the Chief Constable, so it appeared. But this was the Achilles' heel that seemed to afflict all these men. Edward was beginning to wonder if it came with the territory. Was there a correlation between a voracious appetite for wealth and the same propensity for excess elsewhere in life?

What was his own Achilles' heel? He needed to stay alert to his own weaknesses. He was unlikely to be immune from this fatal flaw.

'I think you'll be an asset to our consortium,' Edward said. 'I'm sure you must have met Fred Walker already, maybe at a local fund-raising event?'

'Yes, I know Fred already. He was in the year above me at school. Morecambe is a small town, and I've met most of the movers and shakers at one time or another.'

'Well, look, we'd love to have you on board. Let's get this tender in the bag and then we can talk about numbers. Your investment will help considerably with project cash flow and will allow us to take out profits earlier. That's a good thing for everybody.'

As Barry McMillan shook hands with Edward and headed off for his next appointment, Edward stayed a few minutes longer to finish off his tea. As he sat there mulling over recent events, it had struck him what his own weakness might be. He'd already demonstrated it with Bruce Craven, and it was something that he resolved to keep in check. It was possible, he considered, that in his rush towards wealth and power, he was too quick to trust people. He'd been flattered by Barry's enthusiasm to work with him; he just hoped that none of these relationships would come back to bite him in the future.

CHAPTER THIRTEEN

Morecambe - Present Day

'Will Grayson, to see Charlotte,' he repeated as a nurse's voice came over the security system.

'We're not open for visiting,' the voice responded. It was youthful, a female, perhaps a student or a recent recruit. Will had heard the electronic voice assistants that were appearing in people's houses. This was like speaking to an AI with a bad attitude.

'Yes, I know,' he continued, trying to remain calm and reasonable and still struggling with his words. 'But I... I need to see my wife. It was an emergency... surely the rules don't... don't apply?'

Will heard the beginnings of a conversation. Then the speaker went dead. He wondered if this particular AI had found something more interesting to do. Then there was a buzz to his right-hand side, and the door clicked open.

He walked into the ward, scanning it to see where Charlotte's bed might be. The lighting was dim, and the ward quiet. There were only two nurses at the work station. One was young, the owner of the intercom voice, he assumed. Her companion looked older and more assured; he figured she'd made the decision to allow him to enter.

'Hi, thanks for letting me in. I'll stick to proper visiting times ... from now on... I promise. Where's Charlotte, please?'

They looked at him warily, clocking immediately that his speech was slurred and erratic.

'She's in the far room. She's had the police with her for much of the time. I should think she'll be glad of a break.'

Will thanked them and headed to the far corner. There was space for three beds in the room, but Charlotte had it to herself. She was dozing when Will walked in.

'Hi Charlotte,' he whispered, 'Are you awake?'

'Drowsing,' she answered, cocking one eye open to get a look at him. 'You look terrible, Will. Are you okay? I feel like I should be bringing you flowers and grapes.'

'I've had better days,' Will replied, sitting on the side of the bed and giving her a kiss.

'What's the shiny dress doing here?' he asked, picking up a crumpled garment which had been discarded at the end of the bed.

'Oh, that's DCI Summers' dress. She got changed in my shower room. She was still done up in her charity event gear when she arrived here. Apparently she always keeps a bag of spare clothing in the back of her car for quick costume changes in case she gets called out on a job. Good thinking, or else she'd be stuck in high heels all evening.'

'Anything from Lucia yet?' Charlotte asked. 'I'm sure Kate would have told me if there was.'

'So it's Kate now, is it? You're on first-name terms?'

Will suddenly went dizzy and lurched off the side of the bed, staggering a little before regaining his balance.

'You've got to go to A&E, Will. I can tell you're not right.'

There was a noise from outside near the nurse's station. It sounded like something had been dropped. They listened, ignored it, then carried on speaking.

'How can I, while Lucia's still out there? She could be anywhere.'

'DCI Summers says they're doing everything they can. I'm trying not to go crazy here, but they won't discharge me until tomorrow morning, after I've been checked by a doctor. Olli will be in here for a couple of days, by the sound of things.'

'Where is Olli? I'd like to check on him while I'm here.'

Will remembered why he'd rushed to the hospital. His mind was so foggy. He couldn't believe he'd forgotten.

'Charlotte... those men... they're here in the hospital. Who's with Olli? Does he have a police officer with him?'

'Will, it's okay, DCI Summers is speaking to him now. He's safe.'

'But they're here, I saw them. You're in danger. We're all in danger.'

'Did you get the video, Will?'

'Yes, it's safe with Rex. It's a long story. I have to find DCI Summers. They need to give you protection. I'll ask the nurses where she is.'

Will let go of Charlotte's hand and walked towards the door. The moment he saw the nurse's station, he could tell something was wrong; neither of the nurses was there. Something made him look behind the counter. The young nurse was lying motionless on the floor, her eyes shut. Will's instinct was to vomit. The men had been here.

Without a sound, he ran back to Charlotte's room and turned off the light.

'Be quiet, they're here,' he warned her, suddenly feeling sharper as a result of the adrenaline rush.

'Who's here?' she asked.

'Shh! Keep your voice down. Those men who tried to hurt Olli. The same men who are coming for you. They're here. They must be working their way through the rooms. We have to run.'

Charlotte leapt out of bed. She was wearing a hospital robe. Will noticed the dressings on her arms where she'd stumbled on the rocks and fought to keep upright in the water.

'I've got my phone,' she told him. 'It's got some charge now, I can use it again. We need to call Kate Summers.'

'There's no time,' Will whispered. 'We have to get out of this ward, then we'll call her. Bring your phone; mine is shot. I'll see if the coast is clear.'

Will hadn't taken much notice of the layout of the rooms when he'd walked in, but now it could mean the difference between life and death. As he peered round the side of the door frame, he saw the two men coming out of a room opposite. They were signalling to each other rather than speaking; it looked like they'd done this sort of thing before. They stepped into the corridor and looked around. One of the men seemed to be in charge. He pointed to the room beside the nurse's station. If they were working clockwise, they'd be at Charlotte's room next. Will watched them go through the door opposite then put his hand up as a signal to Charlotte.

'Can you run?' he asked.

'Yes,' she said. 'I'm fine, honestly.'

'We've got to go now. Quiet as you can, they're working their way round the beds. Ready? Let's go.'

Will led the way, with Charlotte following behind him. As they were halfway along the corridor, she dropped her phone. It shattered the silence of the ward.

'Shit, come on, we've got to run!'

'I need my phone...'

'For God's sake, Charlotte, run!'

She picked it up anyway, not daring to look behind her, and blindly followed him.

Will pulled at the door but it was locked. His head was pounding, his legs unsteady.

'Get them, before they can leave the ward!' the man with the

coarse gravelly voice called out from behind them.

Will turned to see a big man running towards them at speed.

'How do we open the fucking door?' he shouted.

Charlotte lurched to one side and thumped a square, metal button that was mounted at the wall at hip height.

'It's unlocked now,' she said.

Will opened the door, let her through, and pushed it closed. A cleaner was working his way along the corridor with a mop and bucket. Will spotted that the bucket was on wheels, so he kicked it as they ran past, sending it flying towards the door of the ward. They ran along the corridor, the curses of the cleaner following them, and heard the second man swear as he tripped over the bucket.

'Where do we go?' Charlotte asked, running alongside Will. He realised she had no footwear on; that could slow them. They came to a junction in the corridor. Will looked from left to right, then took the left-hand fork.

'Down here,' he said, darting to one side and pulling

open a fire door. He staggered a little, losing his balance momentarily. They ran down a flight of stairs and opened the door at the bottom; they had to confuse their pursuers to stand any chance of gaining time. The moment they could place a call to DCI Summers, they would.

'This... this way,' he said, choosing a route at random, forcing his way through the fog in his mind. He could hear the footsteps of the men behind them. At least they didn't have a direct line of sight. This was their chance to get away.

Charlotte followed close behind him. They were both getting out of breath, Will's vision was blurring, and he was struggling to read the signs on the walls. His head still pounded, only more insistently now that the blood was coursing through his veins like a river in flood.

'Over there!' Charlotte pointed towards a door that opened out on to a bins compound.

They'd somehow arrived at the back of the café. It was still open. There was a handful of people there, and Will thought he saw Daisy Bowker, but his vision was so unreliable, he couldn't be certain.

'I can hear them coming,' Charlotte said. 'Quick, let's go behind the bins.'

Will followed her lead this time, grateful that he didn't have to take charge of everything. He was struggling with an overwhelming sensation, as if his brain was conspiring to hijack his body.

They ducked behind one of four large, black industrial bins, all piled high with bags of waste from the cafeteria. The powerful aroma of decomposing food assaulted their nostrils.

'I'll text Kate Summers. I daren't make a call,' Charlotte whispered.

'Good idea. I'll find something in this rubbish to use as a weapon.'

As he moved awkwardly on all fours along the bins, looking for a discarded bottle, Charlotte reached out and touched him. He turned his head to look at her, then followed her gaze. One of the men was standing at the open door from the cafeteria, and he'd just started moving in their direction.

CHAPTER FOURTEEN

Morecambe - Present Day

Will stayed absolutely still as the man moved up to the first bin in the row. He signalled to Charlotte to move into the gap between two of the bins, while he did the same. As she took cover, he caught sight of a dressing on her foot. She'd struggle to run far with nothing to protect her. They'd have to find safety somewhere; her feet would be torn to shreds if she had to run through the streets.

Will heard the grating voice of the man who'd passed him in A&E.

'Anything?' the voice called out. Will couldn't get a clear view, but he guessed the second man was standing by the open door.

'I think they gave us the slip,' the man closest to the bins replied. 'There's nowhere for them to go and we have the all the videos, anyway. The boss told us to leave the son for now. There's too much security around him. Let's just check the ground floor one more time. Then we should head back.'

Will began to breathe again as the voices faded into the distance and the men disappeared through the doorway. Cautiously, he signalled to Charlotte that she should come out of her hiding place.

'They've gone; it's safe,' he whispered. 'We need to get out of here.'

'Where?' Charlotte asked. 'We're best contacting DCI Summers.'

'Yes, but only when we're well away from this place.'

'I'm still in a hospital gown. I can't go anywhere in this.'

For the first time in several hours, Will managed a smile. She looked ludicrous, crouched behind the bins like that, the hospital gown barely covering her.

'Look, take my sweater. I'll be warm enough in a shirt.'

'This has blood on it, Will!'

'Yes. I had a scuffle with your Mohican guy.'

'You saw him? Did he say anything?'

'He was trying to kill me, Charlotte. We need to tell DCI Summers where he is. They should pick him up and question him.'

'Do you have the car?' Charlotte asked.

'Yes, but it's at the other side of the hospital, by the entrance. It doesn't seem a good idea to use it right now. Let's head into town and get a taxi.'

'Where to?'

'I have no idea, Charlotte!' Will snapped. 'I'm sorry, it's just that my head feels like it's on fire. Let's just get out of here, so we can't run into those two guys. We'll take the back streets to the taxi rank at the bus station. We could hide out with Rex; he's safe in that boarded-up shop. DCI

Summers could join us there and we can give her the spare video.'

'Okay, but we need to take care of Rex first. The moment they see him, they'll lock him up and ask questions later. He saved Olli's life, Will, and I'm not prepared to throw him to the lions.'

Will nodded. They both had good reason to thank Rex Emery.

'Okay, come on, let's move while it's still clear,' he said. Charlotte looked passable with his sweater on. It was the early hours of Sunday morning; Lancaster would have seen much worse on a Saturday night.

They passed the canal bridge and took a sharp left, which carried them away from the city's one-way system. Will struggled to remember the layout of the city, working out a route to take them past the castle and the bus station.

They made their way along the pavements, keeping in the shadows, Will checking for glass or any other obstacles which might hurt Charlotte's feet. As they neared the city centre, Will suggested that Charlotte duck out of sight into the entrance of an Olde Worlde pub which had been built from old wine cellars. They'd drunk there as students. It would provide good cover, and he had a plan.

'Where are you going?' Charlotte asked.

'I've just thought of a way to get something for your feet. Wait here and give DCI Summers a call. I'll be back soon.'

Charlotte wasn't happy.

'It's past one o'clock on a Saturday night, and I'm out here in a nightgown and no shoes. I feel vulnerable on my own, to be honest with you. Some drunk might see me and decide to try his luck. I'd rather you stayed.'

'Look, the pub is closed, and this part of town is quieter. I promise I'll only be two minutes.'

Will could see she was still doubtful, but he carried on regardless. There would be charity shops nearby, and people often left bags outside when they were closed. With a bit of luck, somebody might have been having a weekend clearout.

The pavement outside the first charity shop he came to was piled high with kids' toys, as if a tipper truck had been used to get rid of all the junk they couldn't sell at a jumble sale. It reminded him of when Lucia and Olli were small. Today's fad soon became tomorrow's recycling.

He moved on through town, thinking of Lucia as a toddler. He wondered when he and Charlotte had become the enemy to Lucia. She used to tell them everything, but gradually she'd become closed off to them. They spent so much time worrying and fretting about her that sometimes they forgot to love her; she was still just a kid, after all.

Will's mind had drifted again. He needed to stop for a moment and focus his thoughts. Charity shops, that was what he was looking for. On his way along the street, he smiled to himself as he spotted the giveaway pile of bin bags piled against the door outside a Salvation Army shop. He rushed at them like a child tearing at Christmas presents, pulling the contents on to the pavement. He would send the Salvation Army a donation later, to pay for the clothes and make up for leaving such a mess.

He'd hit the equivalent of a tramp's jackpot; this looked like items from a house clearance, including various items of clothing. Will picked out a pair of jeans, a sweater, a tracksuit top, some sports socks and two pairs of casual shoes. He found a bra too; he hadn't a clue what size it was, but Charlotte might appreciate it.

Throwing the items into the remnants of one of the bin bags, he started to run back towards Charlotte. As he began to pick up speed, his head started to pound once again, and his eyesight became blurred. For a moment he felt like he was swimming. He had to stop, centre himself and make certain he was heading in the right direction. He saw the light from Charlotte's phone before he could pick her out in the darkness.

'Charlotte, it's me,' he whispered. She stepped out of the shadows, relieved to see him.

'Your man got away,' she said.

'Who?'

'The guy with the Mohican. DCI Summers sent an officer to pick him up while you were out scavenging for clothes. There was plenty of blood and even a fragment of flesh still on the gate post, but he'd gone by the time they got to him.'

'Damn,' Will cursed. 'Did you tell her what's happened?'

'Of course, I did,' Charlotte said, holding out her hand to take the bag of clothing off Will. 'Keep a lookout and make sure nobody's coming. I'm getting dressed.'

'What did she say?'

'She wants us to come in,' Charlotte replied, then burst out laughing. 'This bra is about five times too big, Will, but thanks for the thought.'

'What do you mean?'

'She says she can keep us safe if we come in and stop doing things on our own. She's promised that Olli won't be left unattended. And she told me she needs to see our evidence. She can't take any action over Edward Callow without it. There's nothing to connect him with what's going on. And she still knows nothing about Rex Emery. He's our secret for now.'

Charlotte looked around, then put on the clothes he'd found for her.

'I'm more comfortable in this junk than I was in my high-heels and dress earlier on,' she said, smiling at Will.

Will had been distracted by a noise up ahead. He waved Charlotte back into the shadows.

'Try the shoes for size; we need to be on our way,' he urged her. She selected the shoes with Velcro fastenings and started to put them on. Will retreated into the arched recess of the pub. Whoever had been lurking across the road was now heading straight for them. They had nowhere to run; they were cornered, and all they could do was wait and see who'd found them.

CHAPTER FIFTEEN

Morecambe - 1984

Edward was leaving nothing to chance with Harvey Turnbull. After the mess-up by Bruce Craven, he wanted to be sure that the thugs Turnbull had recommended were capable of thinking things through. He'd got lucky; if Harvey Turnbull hadn't been on the take, he might have found himself linked to Bruce Craven. It was a clumsy mistake on his part, and he had no intention of repeating it.

Edward had left his car at the adjacent caravan park before walking up to Sandy Beaches Holiday Camp. He'd tagged along with a group who had been out walking along the beach, to avoid being noticed at the security gates. It didn't look like they checked guests in and out; as far as he could see, non-residents were welcome to drink in the bars and spend their money on the camp.

His intention was to get a sense of the place. He'd never driven out as far as Middleton Sands before, but he wanted to see where Bruce Craven was spending his summer.

Harvey Turnbull had tipped him off that Bob Moseley and Neil Carthy would be paying Bruce a visit later that night, after he'd finished his shift in the bar. He hadn't met these men yet, but he wanted to see how they operated. After being let down by Bruce, Edward needed somebody reliable who he could trust to get the job done.

He walked around the holiday camp grounds, watching as the holiday-makers abandoned the crazy golf and tennis courts for the arcades as the night drew in, then migrated en masse into the bars. It was a world which Edward had no experience of. He admired the old tower and stood looking out over the beach. He laughed to himself as he saw the nuclear power station in the distance and wondered what the holiday-makers made of it all. Unlike the sands at Morecambe, the beach was stony and unforgiving. There were pockets of sand to be found, but it seemed an unusual location for a holiday destination.

He decided to work his way through the bars, putting on a baseball cap and his reading glasses to disguise himself, on the off-chance Bruce might spot him. He'd abandoned his usual suit and tie for jeans and T-shirt, looking like any other man who might have been spending a week there. It was unlikely that Bruce would spot him. Edward already knew that there were a few bars on-site, from reading a brochure he'd picked up in the reception area at the Town Hall.

The sound of a Frank Sinatra tune drew him in as he made his way through the camp. He followed it to a bar, checking first to see if Bruce was working there that night, but he walked into a sea of grey hair. This wasn't Bruce Craven's sort of place, so he didn't bother ordering, but left the bar to try the Olde Worlde pub that he'd seen on his way in.

This was the family pub. Walking through the holiday camp, Edward realised what an excellent development opportunity it would make. In his mind, he demolished the tacky arcades, leisure areas, entertainment venues and chalets, and imagined it as an open space with high quality and prestigious housing. The beach wasn't suitable for kids who wanted to build sandcastles all summer, but it was great for exercising dogs and bracing walks by the sea. He reckoned there would be good salaries paid at the nuclear plant just along the shore and that would provide a steady stream of hungry buyers.

His mind began to race at the potential of the place. The days of the traditional seaside holiday were numbered. He made a mental note; if the place ever came up for sale—and providing he managed to land the first deal with the construction of the school—this was a piece of land he'd be interested in developing. Fred Walker could work his magic on it and turn it into a private housing estate.

He was in the family bar now, where the age of the customers was more varied, and this suited him better. After taking a good look to see who was serving and who was collecting glasses, he established that there was no sign of Bruce.

Edward walked up to the bar and ordered an orange juice.

'Does a chap called Bruce Craven work this bar?' he asked the young woman who served him.

'Yeah, sometimes,' she answered as she poured his juice. 'I heard he left suddenly this morning. Not sure why. Nobody saw him after he was in here last night. He was playing pool over there most of the evening. There a row at that table, and Bruce left soon afterwards.'

'Left?' Edward asked. 'As in, left the holiday camp?'

'Yeah, gone. Just like that. Suits me, I get to take his shifts. He was a nasty bugger, anyway. I never liked him.'

'Thanks,' Edward said. 'Keep the change.'

He couldn't see a free table, so he remained standing at the bar. Bruce Craven had left Sandy Beaches? For a moment, he doubted himself. Had he got his days mixed up? No, Harvey Turnbull had said it clearly; they'd be visiting Bruce at midnight after his shift was finished. Bruce Craven wasn't due to disappear until then.

He thought it through. Had Bruce got wind of what was coming? Had somebody tipped him off, and he'd done a runner?

Edward sipped his drink, and as he did so, he realised that his jaw was tight. He gulped down the juice and turned to the girl at the bar.

'How many other bars are there on this holiday camp? Where else do you work shifts?'

'Just the big ship,' she replied. 'It's busy as anything in there at this time of night.'

'The big ship?' Edward asked.

'You can't miss it. It has three giant funnels on top.'

Edward had seen it but hadn't realised it was supposed to be a ship. He'd assumed the funnels were there for air conditioning or ventilation.

It was easy enough to find. The building dominated the holiday camp. As he walked through the doors, he noted that a cursory effort had been made to give the place a nautical feel. There was the occasional ship's wheel mounted on the wall, but nothing else to convey the theme.

A band was playing cover tunes as he walked in. The place was noisy, sweaty and just getting warmed up for an evening of drunkenness. Edward hated places like this, but he could only guess at how much money the bar was taking. He waited in line and ordered a coke. The young barman looked like he might be a student; he was well-spoken.

'Is Bruce Craven here this evening?' Edward asked.

'No, mate,' the barman answered, hardly looking up as he poured the coke. 'They say he left this morning without handing his notice in. He just disappeared without saying a word.'

'Do you know which room he was in?' Edward asked.

'Yeah, sure, he's in the same block as me. Level 2, Grizedale Block, room 10 or 11, I'm not sure of the number. The opposite room has a sticker on the door which says *Home Sweet Home*. It's meant to be ironic, I think.'

'Thanks,' Edward said. He looked at his watch; it was another two hours before Bruce would receive his evening visit from Turnbull's men. It was going to be a long night. Edward bought just one drink in the ship that night, choosing instead to remove himself from the noise and chatter and sit in a quiet reception area instead.

He was happy there, thinking through his plans, working out what he'd do with a large site like Sandy Beaches and content to let his imagination run riot at the potential of a location like that. Away from the noise and mayhem, it seemed no time at all before midnight approached and the drunken revellers began to make their way back to their chalets.

By the time Bob Moseley and Neil McCarthy arrived, Edward was waiting at the bottom of the staircase of Grizedale Block ready to greet them.

'I'm Edward Callow,' he announced, realising who they were at once. They knew him already. It was a good start; they'd done their research.

'Good evening, Mr Callow,' one of the men replied. He

was speaking in a low voice, but he sounded to Edward like he'd been gargling with drawing pins.

'My car is parked across from the entrance to Sandy Beaches at the caravan park. Come and see me there when you're done. I want to know what happens this evening.'

'Will do,' the man replied. This was Bob Moseley, the man who Harvey said had been stabbed in the throat. He wore a shirt which covered the lower part of the neck, presumably concealing a scar.

'I'll leave you to it, gentlemen, and I look forward to receiving your update later.'

Edward made his way back through the camp. It was much quieter now. Nearing the porter's lodge, he saw a man walking towards him, dressed in a uniform. As they got closer, Edward realised that he was one of the security staff. He was annoyed that he'd run into somebody whose job it was to keep the holiday camp safe, but he decided to brazen it out; this man could be useful.

'Good evening,' he said, confident and assured. 'Just on your way to do your rounds?'

'Yes, I always walk the site after throwing out time. It's like checking the doors are locked, and the plugs switched off before you go to bed at home.'

'I don't suppose you've heard of a fellow called Bruce Craven, do you? He had a few music cassettes that he was intending to sell me. He told me to meet him in the bar at the Olde Worlde pub this evening, but I couldn't find him.'

Edward could tell the moment he mentioned the name that this man had heard of Bruce.

'Yes, I know him,' he replied. 'He... well, it was all very unusual. He left the holiday this morning. Slid a note under the door of the admin building and walked out. Didn't collect his pay and didn't say goodbye to anybody. He lives somewhere in Newcastle. I think that might be too far to go to collect a bundle of cassettes.'

Edward laughed. He liked this man.

'You might say that,' he said. 'Never mind... I'm sorry, what's your name?'

'George Newlove,' the man replied. 'Sorry I can't help you.'

'No problem at all,' Edward replied. 'You've been very helpful to me already, thank you.'

CHAPTER SIXTEEN

Morecambe - Present Day

'Well, you two take some keeping up with.'

Will recognised the voice straight away; it was Daisy Bowker.

'How the hell did you find us?' Will asked.

'It's a darned good job I do a bit of running in my spare time,' she said with a smile. 'First, you give me the slip in A&E, then the next thing I know, I'm trying not to give away your whereabouts to a pair of tough guys who look like they're after you. So come on, what's up? And how does this involve my half-brother? The look on your faces when I walked up to you just then... you looked like you were frightened of me.'

'How did you find us?' Will asked.

'I was having a cup of tea in the cafeteria and thinking about catching a taxi back to the guest house when I saw you both creeping by the entrance. I was about to come and see you when two ugly men came along the corridor. They were obviously chasing somebody. I put two and two together and figured it was you they were after. Bearing in mind what's going on with your daughter, it's not hard to figure out that something dodgy is going on.'

Will looked at Charlotte, checking whether she thought it was time to come clean. His head was ready to explode now. If it wasn't for the fact that Lucia was still missing, he would have laid on the floor, curled up into a ball and gone to sleep.

'It seems the time for keeping quiet is over,' Daisy continued. 'Look, I've figured out that Bruce was not well-liked. The mere mention of his name seems to tighten lips and disable tongues. I want to know why. Where is he, and what did he do that makes people hate him so much?'

'Do you mind if I speak to Charlotte?' Will asked. 'Alone, just for a few moments?'

'I understand, you need to get your stories straight. But come on, the next step I take is to ask the police to get involved. As far as I can tell, Bruce Craven is a missing person. He's been missing since 1984!'

Will nodded. Charlotte was fully dressed now.

'I'll walk to the castle and sit on a bench. Come and find me there once you've decided what you're prepared to tell me.'

Daisy set off towards the castle. Will and Charlotte had spent a wonderful afternoon there once as young lovers, not caring where they went, happy to be in each other's company and enjoying exploring the place.

They didn't say a word until she was well out of earshot.

Charlotte was in a state of panic. 'I knew it. She'll speak to the police. I thought we'd get here eventually; that's why I was so wary of the woman.'

Charlotte was in a state of panic. Will couldn't think straight.

'We need to tell her something,' he said. 'Do you think they'll open an investigation after so many years? It'll take them no time at all to start asking us questions. And they already think something's fishy about our time at the camp, because of what happened with Jenna.'

Charlotte's head sank.

'Oh, Will, I don't know. How can we sort this out? We're tangled up in lies. And I still can't see what's happening here. Why is this bloody man still screwing up our lives?'

'The truth will have to be told eventually,' Will said. 'She's too close now. We can't keep brushing her off. I think we need to tell her part of the story. She knows Bruce was unpopular. I say we tell her he was a bully and not well-liked. We mustn't tell her about his relationships...'

Will stopped. He still hated to think of his wife with that man. It made him sick and angry at the same time. So many years, yet the insane resentment still burned strong.

'There are so many people caught up in this: George, Jenna, Abi... Abi has a lot to lose; her daughter Louise is related to Daisy.'

Will waited and listened as Charlotte paused.

'You know, Will, some good might come of all this. Don't forget what Bruce Craven was doing that night. He'd have gone to jail for what he tried to do to us, to all of us. And George is our witness. There are four of us still alive who can confirm what happened that night. Maybe it's time to stare this in the face?'

'Not yet,' Will cautioned. 'Not yet. We need to tell her a part-truth and promise her the rest of the story when we find Lucia. Nothing must put Lucia at risk.'

Charlotte's phone rang. They looked at each other.

'That could be Lucia now,' Will suggested.

Charlotte answered. It was DCI Summers. Charlotte placed her on speakerphone, checking first that nobody was nearby.

'I need you both to come in,' DCI Summers said. 'It's the best thing for your family and your daughter. We've had confirmed sightings of these men you described in the hospital. I believe that you're all in danger. For your own protection, you'll be best in police custody. Two members of the nursing staff on Charlotte's ward were found dead: one strangled, the other stabbed. I'm not sure what you've got yourselves into here, but we need to make sure you're all safe. This is now a murder investigation, and you're both in it up to your ears.'

'How is Olli?' Will asked. 'Is he safe? Are you protecting him?'

'We have two officers posted outside his room. There were reports of two men being seen lurking in the area, but they're off the premises now. From what Charlotte told me about what happened at the stone jetty, she had a narrow escape. I need you where I can see you. I can't let you roam around trying to sort this on your own.'

Will and Charlotte looked at each other. Will glanced up the hill towards the castle. He could see that Daisy was on her way back to them, no doubt waiting for an answer. His vision began to fade again. It was like watching the world through an old fashioned TV on the blink. Still, his head pounded like there was a creature in there trying to break its way out, seeking an escape route.

'We can't do that, DCI Summers, I'm sorry,' Charlotte said.

Will looked at her. She'd just taken an important decision on behalf of both of them. He simply didn't have the energy to carry on, desperately wanting to help Lucia, but with nothing left. He was beaten.

Everything was closing in on them. Daisy Bowker was breathing down their necks, DCI Summers was after them, two nurses were dead because of them, and the man with the purple hair had been ready to kill him with a knife. DCI Summers was right; it was time to call it a day and hand it to the police. With his mind in a dense cloud of fog and his body craving rest, Will decided that it was the best thing.

Daisy Bowker re-joined them, unaware that DCI Summers was on the phone.

'So what's it going to be then? Will you speak to me, or do I go to the police and open up a missing person investigation?'

'Who is that speaking?' DCI Summers asked.

Daisy seemed surprised to hear the disjointed voice, but soon realised she'd walked in on a call.

'You need to tell me where you are,' DCI Summers continued, not getting an answer to her question. 'I'll send out two officers to pick you up straight away. We'll make sure you're safe, and we've doubled our efforts to find your daughter. This is far too dangerous for you to deal with on your own. Charlotte? Will?'

Will could take it no more. The fog in his head had overcome him, he could no longer focus on the phone, and his head now felt like somebody had prised it open and was tearing it apart. He closed his eyes and began to sink into blissful oblivion. He was keeling over, but in a dreamlike state, as if he was imagining it.

He sensed it happening in slow motion until his head

crashed to the pavement. Charlotte's voice was the last thing he heard as he faded away.

'Will? Will? I knew he should have got checked out at the hospital. Oh my God, Will. Is he still breathing?'

CHAPTER SEVENTEEN

Morecambe - Present Day

'Do you know anything about first aid?' Charlotte asked Daisy in desperation. She'd suspected right from the start of the evening that Will wasn't right, but they'd pressed on and ignored it. He'd received a blow to the head, been attacked in the street and had to run for his life through Lancaster. She hated herself for not insisting he seek medical attention.

Daisy was calm as she knelt by Will's side, checking his pulse and his eyelids.

'He's alive, but in a bad way,' she said.

'What's happened, Charlotte? What's going on there? Who's that with you?'

DCI Summers was still on speakerphone. Daisy reached across, took the phone gently from Charlotte's hand and muted the microphone.

'How is this going to play out, Charlotte? I like you, and I like Will, and I don't believe for one moment that you've done anything wrong here. But you've lied to me about my half-brother. So what's it going to be? Shall I tell this police officer—whoever she is—what's going on? Or shall we make sure your husband is safe and sort this thing out together?'

Charlotte looked at Will as he lay on the ground, apparently out cold. She was scared he might have brain damage as a result of his injuries. Who knew what was going on inside his head?

Her priorities were her family. Olli was safe, and Will could be helped soon. That left her free to find Lucia. There was no way she could hand herself in to DCI Summers and just sit there. She would fight for Lucia to her dying breath. It was time Bruce Craven stayed in his grave.

She took the phone from Daisy.

'Get ready to do some more running,' she said. 'I'll tell you what you want to know.'

Daisy released the phone and Charlotte took the speaker off mute.

'I'm sorry DCI Summers, I'm not coming in, not until I'm certain my daughter is safe. When that happens, I'll tell you everything. I need you to trust me. My husband has received a blow to the head. It's serious. He needs urgent attention. In a moment I'll tell you where he is. You won't find me here when you send your officers. The next time you hear from me will be if I find out where Lucia is, and I need your help. The next time I hear from you, you should be telling me you've found my daughter or—'

The words almost stuck in her throat.

'Or you're giving me a medical update on my husband.'

'We can trace your phone,' DCI Summers said. 'I haven't done that yet, but if I have to, I'll set it in motion.'

'Yes you can, but if you do that, I'll switch it off. I don't believe you're that sort of person, DCI Summers. I reckon you're the kind of woman who would walk over hot coals for her family. Am I right?'

'OK, we won't track your phone, I promise. But you're doing the wrong thing, Charlotte. These are dangerous men. I'm telling you one last time; you need to place yourself in police custody. It's the only way I can keep you safe.'

'Get an ambulance to Will,' Charlotte told her. 'Leave your phone on. When I call you next, I'll need you to come fast.'

Charlotte signalled to Daisy that they needed to move. Before getting up, she bent over and gave Will a long, soft kiss. She stood up and began to start jogging up towards the castle, and Daisy followed her lead.

'You'll find Will at the entrance of The Merchants pub. I think he's suffering from concussion, but he's sustained a head injury. Make sure they're aware of it at the hospital. Find my daughter, Kate. Get to her, before I have to.'

Charlotte ended the call, then ran up towards the castle and back down the hill towards the Judge's Lodgings, crossing the road past where her old student bank used to be. It wasn't even a bank any more; so much had changed.

Across the city, she could see the blue lights flashing behind them. They'd got Will; DCI Summers had been as good as her word. Now they had to get back to Morecambe.

Charlotte and Daisy arrived at the bus station to find that there were no taxis at the rank.

'Shit!' she cursed. 'There won't be any buses at this time of night either.'

'We should wait at the taxi rank, in case one comes by,' said Daisy.

'We'd be like sitting ducks there,' Charlotte protested. 'If a cop car comes by, they'll spot us.'

'Well, they're not looking for me,' Daisy pointed out.

'And dressed up in that clobber, I'm not entirely sure they'll recognise you either.'

'I need to get changed if I can. There's a back way into the guest house...'

'They'll be watching the guest house, won't they?'

'You'll still be able to come and go. I'll give you the key. You can get me one of Olli's caps and a pair of shoes that fit. Then we need to get that video off Rex Emery.'

'We?' Daisy asked.

'I'll tell you about Bruce if you help me. Believe me, we're the only ones who can tell you the truth about your half-brother. And you have to promise not to speak to the police, not until Lucia is safe.'

'I promise,' Daisy said. 'I'm not after blood here, Charlotte. I just want people to stop telling me lies. For all I know, my brother was a paedophile. I want the truth.'

'Here's a taxi,' Charlotte said, putting out her hand to get the driver's attention. 'Do you have any money?'

'Yes; this is the most expensive stay at a guest house I've ever had.'

Charlotte glanced at her and was relieved to see she'd said it with a smile.

'Drop us off outside the Town Hall in Morecambe,' Charlotte said to the driver. 'That'll be close enough, in case there are police officers there.'

'So, we've got a ten-minute journey back to Morecambe. I'm a captive audience. Tell me about Bruce.'

Charlotte's phone beeped with a text from DCI Summers, confirming they'd got Will. She was torn between wanting to be with Will and Olli and desperately needing to know that Lucia was safe. Every time she thought about her daughter, anxiety raged through her body. But now she had a plan.

Charlotte looked at Daisy.

'Okay,' she began. 'You're right, we knew Bruce. We wanted to spare you the truth. He was a nasty man. One day, he burned Will's hand for no reason by holding it under boiling water, and another time he attacked us. He was a violent, aggressive man who wasn't well-liked, unless you were one of his cronies.'

Daisy was silent for a few moments.

'I thought as much,' she muttered. 'What was his connection to Abi?'

Charlotte had no intention of telling the whole truth, not yet.

'We all worked together and socialised together. Abi would have known Bruce from the kitchens and perhaps later in the bars. He used to be on the dishwashing crew. Later he got promoted to bar work. We didn't see much of him after that.'

'Who was that woman in the photo, the one taken by the paddling pool? He looked like he was close to her. Did he have girlfriends?'

Charlotte was pleased that the only light available was coming from the occasional street lamp along the road; she could feel her cheeks burning up.

'I'm sure Bruce must have had girlfriends, but I can't recall any of them.'

She thought back to Jenna. Poor Jenna. She prayed that she was okay. Piper too. What a mess this whole thing was. It was screwing up all their lives, and Daisy wanted to know more about it.

'What happened to him?' Daisy asked. 'Where did he go? He can't have just disappeared.'

'That's just it; he did,' Charlotte said. Only four of them

knew the truth. Everybody else at the time assumed he'd gone.

'It's true. He left one day and we never saw him again. All the staff were talking about it. The night before, I noticed him in the bar playing pool. He must have left at some point. At the breakfast shift the next day, everybody was gossiping about it, saying Bruce Craven had handed in his notice and left the holiday camp. No reason, no explanation, he'd just gone. Everybody assumed he'd had enough. It was crappy work and crappier wages. In those days, people used to come and go all the time, as casual workers. That was the last we saw of him. I didn't like him, I'm sorry to say, but no one did. And that's it, that's all I can tell you about Bruce Craven.'

'That's interesting. It confirms what Abi Smithson was telling me earlier on this evening.'

'Exactly!' Charlotte replied, relieved that it tied in with everything Abi had told her. Abi would never tell Daisy about her daughter. She had her own reasons for hating Bruce Craven, and she'd be as eager as the rest of them to keep Daisy Bowker at a distance.

For a few moments, Charlotte believed that she'd given Daisy enough information to stop her from pushing any further. But Daisy had one more question that she wanted to ask.

'So how come she let slip that you and Bruce used to be an item? Why didn't you bother to mention that bit?'

CHAPTER EIGHTEEN

Morecambe - 2006

'Just remember Harvey: you don't lay bricks, you don't operate diggers, and you don't push wheelbarrows. Your contribution to these projects is tenuous and it has been since 1984. So get back in your box and be grateful that you're still part of this good thing we have going on.'

Edward Callow was furious. They were all rich men as a result of their success, but Harvey Turnbull had ceased to contribute anything useful for a long time. The problem was that they'd gone legit. The days of intimidating council-lors who exposed themselves and needing to convince committees that Fred Walker's company was big enough to cope were long gone.

Harvey Turnbull had been vital in those early days. He and his two fixers had done good work, lurking in the shad-ows, leaving a trail of fear and doubt behind them, making sure that nothing ever surfaced that could bring the entire house of cards tumbling down.

These days people actively sought out Fred Walker to deliver big contracts. If you had a massive infrastructure project, if you needed a complex building delivered and completed on time and on budget, you made a specific request for Fred Walker. All five men had got rich from it, but now Harvey Turnbull wanted more.

'I know things that could put you in jail, Edward. You may well be our new MP, but imagine if some of the things we've done got out into the public arena.'

'Are you threatening me?' Edward asked. He'd calmed his voice now. If he shouted, he'd lost the argument.

'I'm not threatening you,' Harvey replied. 'I'm only suggesting that you might review the value I bring to the party.'

'And what value is that?' Edward asked. 'I agree, in the early days, you were a key component in getting our business underway. But now? It's a long time since I needed your services. And in twelve years, you and your hapless bobbies have been unable to tell me what happened to that Bruce Craven fellow. He's the one stray bullet who could take us out. People don't just disappear. You of all people realise that. They get killed, and their bodies are disposed of. Or they kill themselves, and their bodies don't get found. Somebody knows what happened to that idiot, and until we close the lid on this, it's the last thing that could come back to bite us. Solve that problem for me, and I'll renegotiate your cut.'

'I've told you, it's a cold case. We're not opening a formal investigation because nobody ever reported him missing. It would be a crazy thing to do. I've spoken to contacts at Newcastle, and they have nothing on the man. As far as the police are concerned, he doesn't exist. All that's left is a National Insurance number. He is unofficially a missing person. He's gone, Edward, I'm telling you, and if it's good enough for me as a copper, it should be good enough for you. You scratch that itch and I'm warning you, you'll stick your hand in a hornet's nest.'

'Look, let's both go away and think about this, Harvey. We need to cool down. This partnership has continued to work well because we all take equal shares. If we start showing favouritism, Mason and Barry may become a problem. Let's not upset the applecart.'

'You know what those two are up to, I take it? Mason is getting worse. We need to keep an eye on him. There's only so much I can do to keep him away from my colleagues. One complaint from an angry parent and it'll get out of hand. Do you think for one moment that Mason Jones will keep his mouth shut under pressure of police questioning? He's been getting Barry involved too.'

'You're kidding,' Edward replied. One thing he'd learnt in twelve years of co-managing infrastructure projects was that people were a pain in the arse. Mason Jones was needy and unreliable, and Barry McMillan was intoxicated by the power of his fame and money. Fred Walker, thank God, was still happy to turn up for the newspapers and get photographed shovelling concrete and laying bricks. He'd had two more affairs, according to Harvey's spies, but he was committed to keeping his original family together and had no intention of moving in with any of his female dalliances.

'I wish I was joking. It seems like Mason has got Barry into younger girls. I think he likes the excitement and thrill of it. The sixth formers tolerate it because of the money they can earn; it's a lot more lucrative, giving some dodgy bloke a blow job than working ten hours a day in the arcades. It'll only take one of these kids to speak, and we'll have to be all over them. There's only so much influence I have; I can't put a stop to a formal investigation.'

Edward gave a sigh of frustration. 'Why the hell can't everybody just enjoy the money we're making and keep their zips up? Is it so difficult?'

'When you've dealt with Morecambe's low-life as long as I have, you've seen it all. Believe me, there's nothing you can imagine, no scenario that you can dream up, that some weirdo or other hasn't indulged in. At least Barry and Mason are with kids who are of legal age. So long as they remain in that grey area, and the kids are happy to earn more pocket money than they've ever earned in their life, it will all be sweet. You don't have anything I need to know about, do you Edward? There's nothing in your life that might cause any problems?'

If there was one thing that Edward Callow could rely on, it was himself. He'd remained unmarried, having discovered as he'd moved into his mid-thirties that he could live without female or male companionship. Intimate relationships didn't interest him. They seemed to complicate life too much. He'd never been engaged, never had a serious girlfriend and was not hiding any secrets about his sexuality in a secure closet. He simply wasn't interested. The infrastructure projects and his life in parliament were engaging, and there was no room in his life for anything else.

He looked at Harvey Turnbull and was pleased that he'd taken a more conciliatory tone now. What the man needed was a big case to distract him. He was bored, rich and needed something more to take up his time. The same was true of Barry and Mason. Every book that Barry released brought more accolades and new deals; it seemed he could do no wrong. In his own way, Mason Jones was also at the height of his powers; head of a successful, new secondary school and an adviser to the government on a range of education issues. Even Fred Walker had it sorted; he hadn't got his hands dirty in several years, other than for photo shoots. He too was bored and seeking distraction in the form of affairs.

Edward was pleased that he'd avoided this idleness in his own life; it was self-destructive. But he resolved to keep a closer eye on his business partners. There was no way he would let any of them jeopardise what he'd worked so hard to build up.

CHAPTER NINETEEN

Morecambe - Present Day

The taxi driver's timing was perfect.

'That'll be six pounds and forty pence, my darling,' he said, turning to face them. It gave Charlotte the couple of minutes she needed to recover. She cursed Abi's big mouth, then decided to cut her some slack. Abi had no reason to conceal that information, because she was never involved directly in the events of that night, even though she'd set the argument in motion in the bar that night.

It had been Abi's drunken behaviour that had caused Charlotte to storm out, setting off the fateful sequence of events which resulted in Bruce's death. Abi would have been in her bed, sleeping off a hangover while everything played out, knowing nothing about it. So perhaps it was understandable that she thought it perfectly harmless to tell Daisy that Charlotte and Bruce had briefly been an item.

'What did Abi tell you?' Charlotte asked. It seemed the

safest course of action. Find out what she knew and frame a lie around it.

'Only that you and Bruce were boyfriend and girlfriend for a short time.'

They were standing on the pavement opposite the Town Hall now, the taxi driver having driven off.

'Well, that's all there is to say,' Charlotte continued, relieved that Abi hadn't gone into any detail. 'When I first met Bruce, he seemed charming and good-looking, in a macho kind of way. I was only eighteen. I was young and naïve, and I hadn't had a proper boyfriend. Will was my first serious boyfriend. I soon found out that Bruce was a nasty piece of work. When I met Will, he threatened him, warning him to stay away from me. That's when I decided to end it. It was a brief and meaningless holiday fling. I'd forgotten about it. It's so long ago now.'

'Why didn't you tell me?' Daisy asked. They hadn't started walking back towards the guest house yet.

'I didn't want to disappoint you,' Charlotte replied. It looked like Daisy believed this latest account. The less she could give away, the better. 'Bruce Craven disappeared out of our lives well over three decades ago. He was nasty, violent and horrible to be around. As soon as I discovered that about him, we split up and not long after he left the holiday camp. I don't know what happened to him after that and I don't care. I told you, he left the camp, and that was the end of it.'

'So who is Jenna?' Daisy replied after a silence. Charlotte wished she'd let it drop. There were more important matters to deal with. But she needed Daisy. Her rental car would come in useful for her next stop-off.

'Abi mentioned Jenna?' Charlotte asked.

'She's in the photograph that Jon Rogers showed me, the one taken by the paddling pool at the holiday camp.'

'There's nothing much to say,' Charlotte continued, after an uncomfortable gulp which she hoped Daisy hadn't noticed. 'Jenna and I were friends from college. When I finished with Bruce, she had a brief relationship with him. We were both young and daft around men. She should have known better, but I think she needed to find out for herself. Bruce would have been attractive to women if you were into that sort of thing. I thought I was, then found I preferred gentle guys like Will. Jenna was seeing Bruce when he left the camp—'

She stopped talking, realising she'd said a little too much. She should have closed the door on Jenna, but instead, she'd opened one up.

'So Jenna would have been one of the last to see him? He might have told her he was going?'

'Oh no, I don't think so,' Charlotte interrupted, keen to close this down. 'Jenna was as surprised as the rest of us. I don't think she even saw him before he left.'

'Where's Jenna now?' Daisy asked. Charlotte felt like a Rottweiler had bitten into her leg and wouldn't let go. The questions were coming too fast.

'I'm not sure. We lost touch after college.'

'Abi seemed to think she was still living locally. She said she'd had trouble with the law and that I should discuss that with you, as you might think it was a private matter. There's something you're not telling me, Charlotte. Why won't you say?'

Charlotte snapped.

'For Christ's sake Daisy, will you drop it! I've told you the truth about Bruce, and everybody you ask will tell you the same thing. He was a horrible man. There was no love lost for him, and I was pleased to see the back of him. I regret the day I ever saw that man. If only I'd met Will a month earlier, Bruce would never have come into my life. Will and I would have got together, and that would have been it. Your half-brother is a blot on our relationship; didn't you ever consider that's why I might not want to talk about him?'

She could see from Daisy's face that she was on the back foot now, so she carried on with that line of attack.

'Will was jealous of Bruce, and it wasn't the best of starts to our relationship. It still riles him all these years after. Didn't you have previous boyfriends? Did your husband know about them? And if he did, how much did he enjoy hearing about them?'

'Well, I just thought—'

Charlotte had her now.

'If you want more information, find Jenna and speak to her yourself. I've told you what I know. I'd be grateful if you respected my relationship with Will and didn't keep prying into sensitive topics.'

Daisy was quiet now.

'Can we get back to finding Lucia please?' Charlotte asked.

Daisy nodded.

'I still think you're hiding something, but I'll find this Jenna, as you suggest, and ask her. She might know what happened in those final hours before he left. Maybe they had a row?'

'Maybe,' Charlotte answered. She'd shaken the Rottweiler off her leg, and she was grateful for it. 'Now, I want you to check out the front of the guest house for police surveillance. If it's clear, I'd like you to go in and fetch me some footwear. I'd also appreciate a cap and a hairband.

Then I'd like to use your hire car. I have to find my daughter, and we've wasted a lot of time here talking about nothing.'

It looked like Daisy was about to raise a protest, but she stopped short.

'If George and Isla are still awake, tell them what's going on. I want you all to stay put in case Lucia gets in touch.'

'Where are you going?' Daisy asked.

'I can't tell you,' Charlotte replied. 'But I need you to be at the guest house where I can get a message to you. Somebody needs to be ready to welcome Lucia if she comes home. Will you please do that for me, Daisy?'

She nodded.

'Here's the front door key, the key to our living accommodation and key to the back door; they're all clearly marked. Don't tell George and Isla I'm here; they'll only fuss. I want you to get me a change of clothing, and I'll meet you out the back, in the alley. Bring your key for the hire car. I promise I won't damage it. I'm sure my own insurance will cover me to drive.'

'I've got a waiver on it. You'll be fine, I'm certain of it. Please don't get a speeding ticket though; they'll send it to me.'

As they passed the Town Hall grounds and reached Charlotte's terrace, she broke off from Daisy and headed along the short path to the alley at the back of the houses.

'I'll be outside at the back,' Charlotte whispered. She checked her phone. Her power was running low again, it was the curse of having an old device. She was unwilling to use the torch function, wanting to spare the remainder of the battery for as long as possible. She felt for the charger that Will had given her. She swore as she realised she must have left it behind when they were fleeing from the hospital.

The alley was dark and poorly lit. She counted the back yards until she reached the guest house. There were no signs that the rear of the house was being monitored; it felt safe enough to walk into the yard.

There was a single guest car parked there. It looked too old to be a hire vehicle. Daisy must have parked up at the front after coming back from Abi's performance. It might cause an issue if there were cops at the front of the guest house.

As Charlotte lurked in the shadows at the back of the building, she noticed something unusual about the cellar window. Rex Emery had told her he'd used the metal drain-pipe at the back of the house to escape from his room. So why did the window look like it was open? She moved up closer to investigate. As she did so, she heard a key being inserted into the back door. She stepped back into the shadow cast by the high wall along the boundary of the yard.

'Charlotte?' Daisy whispered. She had a plastic carrier bag in her hand.

Charlotte stepped forward, spotting the look on Daisy's face.

'What is it?' she asked. 'Somebody has been in the house, haven't they?'

'Daisy nodded.

'How did you know?'

Charlotte pointed to the window.

'I'm sorry Charlotte, they've ransacked your family quarters. George and Isla were in the lounge at the time. They didn't even hear it. Whatever they were looking for, they gave it a thorough going over. What do you want me to do?'

Charlotte thought a moment.

'Call DCI Summers and get her and her team here, but only after I've had time to get well away. They might get fingerprints or another clue as to the identity of these people. She said she needed evidence, so let's see if she can find some.'

'And you're still intent on going it alone?'

'I have to, Daisy. I can't tell you where I'm going, in case you reveal it to the police. But if DCI Summers asks, tell her I'm going to get my daughter.'

CHAPTER TWENTY

Morecambe - Present Day

Charlotte changed into her own clothes in the back yard, pleased to be out of the uncomfortable, stale clothing that Will had found for her. Daisy had brought socks and a bra, too. Wearing her own clothing made her feel more like herself again. The shoes made the biggest difference.

'Where's the car parked?' she asked.

'It's across the road from the guest house, almost opposite. I don't think the house is being watched. George and Isla agreed with me; they've seen the police drive by from the lounge window, but they don't think anybody is out there.'

'You didn't tell them I'm here?'

'No, they think I went back to my room. Besides, they're upstairs in your family accommodation, assessing the damage. I told them I've called the police. I suggest you make your move. Are you sure I can't persuade you to let the police deal with this?'

'They've been trying, and look how far that got us. No, I'm doing this alone. I'll call the police the moment I get proof. In the meantime, I have some investigating of my own to do.'

Charlotte bundled up her hair into the tie that Daisy had brought, then folded the ponytail up into one of Olli's caps. The disguise would have to do; at least anybody seeking a middle-aged brunette with long hair wouldn't make the connection.

Daisy handed her the keys.

'It's one of these modern locking systems; it unlocks when you walk up to it, and you don't have to insert the key to start the car. It's weird at first, but it works well enough.'

'Thanks, Daisy.' Charlotte said. She meant it too. 'I promise, we'll talk more about Bruce when this is finished. You must understand that Lucia is my priority right now? But we'll do it soon, honestly.'

Daisy nodded, and Charlotte headed off back into the alleyway. Despite Daisy's assurances, she wanted to be certain that nobody was watching the guest house from the road. As she entered the promenade from the side road, she scanned the few cars that were parked opposite the houses. There was no sign of anybody in any of the vehicles.

She crossed the road and walked past the cars, as if she were a passing pedestrian, tilting her head to peer inside. The coast was clear. She'd heard Daisy's hire car unlocking as she passed by, so she opened the door, stepped inside and looked for the start button. After playing with the dashboard controls to figure out where the lighting controls were, she was soon on her way, driving along the sea front.

No wonder it was quiet at that time. The clock on the car's dashboard showed it was almost 2am. At least the hire car wouldn't flag any police checks or alert the men who'd chased them out of the hospital. She was as invisible as she could possibly be.

Charlotte parked the car at the side of West End Gardens, where she'd dropped the video earlier that night. It felt like hours ago; so much had happened since then. She was still sore and stiff from her struggles to rescue Olli from the incoming tide, and her breathing was more difficult than usual, after battling so long with the water to keep it out of her lungs. She'd be better off in the hospital, like Will and Olli. But if she stepped aside, who would sort this out? Not DCI Summers, that was for sure. Kate Summers had to stick to processes and procedures. But Charlotte didn't have to.

She walked towards the shop Will had described, where Rex Emery was hiding. She looked up and down the road, making sure the coast was clear before inserting her fingers into the sides of the chipboard that covered one of the shop windows. It slid off in her hands. Carefully, she stepped inside the building and replaced the chipboard.

She took her phone out of her pocket and switched on a torchlight long enough to work out where she should be walking. Some areas had missing floorboards removed, so she had to pick her route carefully to the bottom of the staircase.

'Rex?' she whispered. 'It's me, Charlotte. Are you there?'

She heard floorboards creaking upstairs, near the back of the building.

'Rex?' she whispered again.

Slowly, she crept up the stairs, pausing on each step to listen. Eventually, she reached the landing.

'Rex?' she ventured, once again.

The door of the room furthest away was open. That must be where the creaking sounds had come from.

She was reluctant to use the torch on her phone, but it was so dark, she had to risk running her battery down. She cursed herself again for leaving Will's power pack behind. The beam shone into the room, and her heart skipped a beat as a shadow on the wall moved. She flinched, dropping her phone.

'Jesus, you scared the life out of me!'

It was Rex Emery.

'Then we're quits. You frightened me too,' Rex replied. He was holding a hammer in his hand.

'You weren't about to hit me with that, were you?'

'Let's put it this way, it's a good job it was just you,' Rex answered.

Charlotte picked up her phone and switched off the torch.

'What are you doing here?' Rex asked. 'Did Will make it back to the hospital? In fact, what are you even doing here? Aren't you supposed to be recovering?'

'It's a long story,' Charlotte began. 'I need your help, Rex. And I have to be sure that video is safe. Is it?'

'Yes, I've hidden it in the loft space for now. It's to the right of the hatch, underneath the insulation material that runs along the joists. I nearly broke my neck, getting it up there. I found an old biscuit tin that the workmen had been using, for extra protection.'

'You're sure it's safe?' Charlotte asked.

'As sure as I can be. Why?'

'We're paying Edward Callow a late-night visit. It's the only way to end this.'

Even in the darkness, Charlotte could sense Rex staring at her.

'You're joking,' he replied at last. 'You saw what he did to Piper. You had to rescue your own son tonight, so you've seen what lengths these people will go to. And now you want to knock on Edward Callow's front door and ask him what he's up to?'

'Not quite. We're going to break into his house.'

'Jesus, Charlotte! Have you gone crazy?'

'Probably. But I am not going to sit here while they have Lucia. I can't even think about her, because I'll go out of my mind imagining the things they might be doing to her. I have to find her, Rex. These men must be acting on Edward Callow's instructions. I'll bet all those video copies are sitting in Callow's house right now. If we move fast, we'll be able to get to them before he destroys them.'

'What good will that do? We have our own copy.'

'What's on that video? Do you even know?'

Rex nodded. 'Yes. It shows a meeting of some sort going on at the guest house. It was recorded in 2006. It looks like the camera was concealed. You can hear voices and some of the conversation.'

'So it doesn't show Edward Callow?'

'No, not directly, he's off camera most of the time. But it loosely connects him to what was going on within the consortium members.'

'I'm not sure it will be good enough,' Charlotte told him. 'Edward Callow faked his own heart attack this evening to throw the police off the scent. He'll be in all the newspapers tomorrow, according to Will. Everybody will be celebrating his fast recovery. He's distancing himself from what's been going on, can't you see? All these deaths... he's cleaning up a mess, if you ask me. And somehow, we've become part of that mess.'

'Okay, but do we have to break into his house? We're playing with fire.'

'We're already in the heart of the fire, if you haven't noticed? You're on the run, and in fear for your life, my daughter is who-knows-where, and my family is in danger the moment the police turn their backs. The cops won't tackle Edward Callow without evidence. He's an MP, so if they get that wrong they'll lose their careers. It's time for a bit of vigilante justice. We're getting the evidence DCI Summers needs, and then we're going after my daughter.

Rex was silent in the darkness. She wished they had some light; it was hard to judge his mood without being able to see his face properly.

'You want to prove your innocence, Rex? We have to do this. Tonight... now, before he destroys any evidence. We need to catch him red-handed with those videos and force him to tell us where Lucia is. I can't wait for the police; Lucia needs me.'

'Okay, I'm in,' Rex said at last. 'We'll need this if things get rough in there,' he continued.

'I can't see,' Charlotte said, 'What are you talking about?'

'Will left this hammer earlier on; I think he baulked at taking a weapon. Well, this time we're not going empty-handed. If I have to use this thing on Edward Callow, I will.'

CHAPTER TWENTY-ONE

Morecambe - 2006

Edward Callow was not a happy man. Bruce Craven was meant to have been dealt with many years ago, and now here was Harvey Turnbull informing him that a man who was supposed to be dead was now the subject of an active police investigation. This was not a conversation that could take place in a local hotel, Barry's amusement arcade or even The Battery.

He looked out over the bay, towards the Cumbrian hills. Somewhere in the distance were Ulverston, Barrow and Grange-over-Sands. He'd lived in the area for more than two decades now, but he was still uncertain of the local geography. Some local people could stand on the sea front and identify the hills on the horizon, but not Edward. To him, this was simply a nice view; his mind was always on other matters.

He'd arranged to meet Harvey opposite the Town Hall, at the quieter end of the promenade. They'd be able to chat freely there, and Harvey would be able to walk over from the police station on his lunch hour. Edward liked to see the Town Hall again. It reminded him how far he'd travelled since he left the planning department and begun his new life.

Edward was intent on cleaning up the business. The days of intimidation were at an end, and he was now over-seeing a legitimate operation. But what had happened in the past couldn't be easily forgotten. And the business part-ners who he once relied upon were becoming albatrosses. Harvey Turnbull, in particular, was bothering him.

He sat on a bench, listening to the waves lapping in the distance. Seagulls were performing feats of aeronau-tics by staying almost motionless in the air even as the wind blew, and dilapidated fishing boats were bobbing in the water as the sea came in. Edward felt in his pockets for his gloves; it could be so cold at times. He was tempted to take refuge in Rex Emery's guest house, which was less than five minutes walk away. But this conversa-tion had to be conducted without the risk of being overheard.

Five minutes later than they'd agreed, Harvey Turnbull arrived, shivering.

'Couldn't you think of somewhere warmer to meet?' he asked.

'It's bitterly cold, I agree,' Edward replied. 'Why didn't you bring a coat? You know how cold it gets out here.'

'I left it in the car. Anyway, we're not here to talk about the weather. You got my message, I take it?'

'Yes. This is not the news I want to hear, Harvey. You assured me the matter of Bruce Craven was dealt with.'

'It was,' Harvey continued. 'These are exceptional circumstances, though. It's unusual for a cold case like this to be re-opened. But it seems somebody's conscience got the better of him.'

'Can we deal with it directly?' Edward asked, speaking to himself as much as Harvey.

'There's no point now; the cat is out of the bag. I can make it go away at our end. But if the cops in Newcastle unearth anything, this is likely to blow up in our faces.'

Edward looked out across the bay once again. One of the things he hadn't expected when he gathered together his small group of collaborators was how much time he would have to spend dealing with people. It was like he was head of the HR department. Somebody was always moaning about something, raising a problem or—even worse—causing one. He'd never expected this. In his imagination, it was much simpler: make money, bank money, make more money. Rinse and repeat.

'Remind me what happened in 1984. You assured me then that this wouldn't be a problem.'

Harvey rubbed his hands. Edward didn't care if he was cold; he had to be sure that this wasn't coming back to bite them.

'You know for yourself what the story was back then. Everybody on that holiday camp said the same thing. Craven was last seen rushing out of the family pub after last orders were called. Nobody saw him after that. The next day, he posted a note under the admin building door, informing them he'd resigned. You heard it yourself, the same night Bob Moseley went out there to finish him off.'

'What about the girl? The one who he was seeing at the time?'

'Jenna Phillips. She's still living locally. Her life is a bit of a mess by all accounts. She has a daughter, a teenager. There's no father on the scene.'

'Was she telling the truth that night?'

'Bob scared the shit out of her. She confirmed exactly what everybody else said. You told us yourself. We checked the family house at Jesmond; nobody lived there. The post was piled up high at the door, and Bruce hadn't been there. If he had, he didn't touch anything. He's gone. Don't ask me where, the man completely vanished.'

'Was he working for anybody else? Is there any chance someone else might have disposed of him? Could he have gone abroad?'

'Look, Edward, Bruce Craven wasn't the sharpest tool in the box; we both know that. He wasn't employed for his intellect. And by the way, just to remind you, he was your first appointment, nothing to do with me. He was your mistake. I just mopped up your mess.'

Edward felt his hackles rising. With Mason, Barry and Fred it was always clear who was boss, but with Harvey, it always seemed like a tussle. He was tired of locking horns with this man, yet he still needed his services. For a while, at least.

'Where's this new investigation come from?'

He decided not to fight with Harvey; he would pursue a longer-term strategy, but it would need to wait for the time being.

'An old friend of Bruce Craven's is dying of cancer in the brain and he's not going to be here much longer. He decided to make a confession before he died. He's a good Catholic most of the time, but it seems he had a little lapse when he got involved in a job for Bruce.'

Edward shuffled on the bench and held up his hand to stop Harvey from talking. An elderly woman was walking by with a small dog. It was a race to see who could walk slowest. The tiny animal looked exhausted by the exercise and the old lady didn't seem to be faring much better. Once they'd passed by, Edward invited Harvey to continue.

'This pal of Bruce's was a gas engineer. It turns out Bruce paid him to overlook a problem with the heater in the sitting room of his parents' house. It was releasing carbon monoxide. Bruce told him they couldn't afford to fix it, and that he'd tell his parents to keep the room ventilated until they could pay to get it repaired.'

'Don't tell me? It never got repaired?'

'No. And it killed both of his parents.'

'Accident? Or murder?'

'Well, that's what my colleagues from Newcastle are trying to find out. So, after all these years, somebody is looking for Bruce Craven. Imagine what it must be like to be gone for so long and have nobody miss you.'

That comment gave Edward pause for a moment. He had no wife, no family and no close friends. His life was all business and politics. Would he be missed? He would build his legacy in bricks and mortar; it was much less transient.

'What about the guy with cancer?'

'Well, he has nothing to lose now; it's not like he needs his job any more. But it turns out he shared it in confession, and his priest advised him to come clean when they were making funeral arrangements from his hospital bed. It's all a bit grim. I take it you don't want me to send him a Get Well Soon card?'

Harvey Turnbull's gallows humour never failed to offend Edward. Life was a series of decisions and transactions, and while this man's confession gave them a problem, he didn't wish him any ill-will. The poor man's manner of death would be punishment enough, regardless of whether he was destined for hell or not.

'So what are you proposing?' Edward asked. If there

was one thing he could rely on Harvey Turnbull for, it was that he always had a solution up his sleeve, usually in the form of Bob Moseley.

'The only link between us and Bruce Craven, given that the man is either dead or untraceable, is Jenna Phillips. Conveniently, she has a daughter, and if there's one great way of finding out the truth, it's to threaten the kids. It works every time. If Jenna wasn't telling us the truth, we'll soon find out.'

'What are you proposing? I don't want any comeback on this, Harvey.'

'Well, it's a neat little plan, to be honest with you. Jenna's daughter will be disappearing for a few days...'

'We're not harming a child, Harvey.'

'She'll come to no harm. And we even get to use Mason's unfathomable abilities to charm just-legal teenagers from the trees. He'll deliver her into Bob Moseley's hands.'

'You'd better be sure this is watertight. I don't want any cock-ups with this.'

'It's fine, Edward, we have it all worked out. We won't need to detain Jenna's daughter for long, just long enough to scare the life out of Jenna. Then we can make sure she wasn't holding anything back the last time we paid her a little visit.'

CHAPTER TWENTY-TWO

Morecambe - Present Day

Charlotte decided that she and Rex should walk to Edward Callow's house. It was fifteen minutes at most, and there would be no car to dispose of. With her hair now contained in Olli's cap, she had a low profile. Besides, in the early hours of Sunday morning, the activity from the previous night's drunkards would have died down. The chances of being spotted by the police were low, but still, she suggested that they walk the back streets to get there.

'What was prison like?' Charlotte asked as they walked. She kept her voice low, not wanting to disturb any residents who might peer out from behind their curtains to see what was going on. It was a subject which she'd often considered at different intervals throughout her life: what was prison life like for a regular person?

'Horrible,' Rex replied, 'but not in the way that everybody thinks. People make jokes about not bending down in the showers, but it's not like that. Most of the guys in there can't read or write. They have wives, girlfriends and kids, and a lot of them were just trying to make ends meet when they became involved in criminal activity. They were earning money the only way they knew how, by stealing or cheating. Sure, you get the psychos in there too, but you give them a wide berth. Most of the guys in there are illiterate. I taught several men how to read, and I wrote letters home for just as many. It's almost like there's an 'us and them' situation. They all realised I was no crook, so I got left alone. I rubbed along nicely most of the time. The real punishment was beyond the prison walls.'

'What do you mean?' Charlotte asked, checking the street names and trying to stay parallel with the main road. Rex had already addressed her greatest fear of constant threat and violence.

'My wife and daughter turned their backs on me. And they ran the business down, after we'd worked so hard to build it up.'

For the first time, Charlotte considered how galling it must have been to see her own family occupying the place where he once made his living.

'That was the hardest part. And knowing that I was innocent and had been stitched up. That was my real prison sentence, and I've had a lot of time to think about it. But if Callow and his cronies get their comeuppance, at least justice will have been done. It won't have all have been for nothing.'

'Why are they doing this to my family?'

It was the one piece of the puzzle that Charlotte couldn't place. How had they got involved in this? Daisy Bowker was a separate matter altogether.

'I can't tell you,' Rex answered after a while. 'All I remember is that things were uneasy back then, about the time Piper was abducted. It all looked smooth on the surface, but there were tensions among Edward's group. I would hear him and Harvey Turnbull arguing in the lounge. I couldn't hear what they were saying, but I got the sense of it. Callow was scared; I think he thought the game was up. Whatever was going on, they wanted to scare Jenna Phillips out of her wits. There was something she knew— was connected with—that was causing Edward to worry.'

Charlotte had to find out what the link was between them all.

'Did you ever know a man called Bruce Craven?'

'The name doesn't ring a bell, but it was a long time ago. What was he like?'

A chill ran through Charlotte's body. She'd spent far too much time thinking about that man.

'He had tattoos on his arms, and he was built like an iron girder. He was attractive, in a basic sense. Think Sean Bean, not conventionally good looking.'

'I've a good idea who you mean.' Rex said after a pause. 'I only ever saw him once or twice. One minute he was on the scene, the next he wasn't.'

'When was this, can you remember?'

'1984,' Rex replied. 'Why?'

Was this the connection?

'We knew him in 1984. He worked at the Sandy Beaches Holiday Camp. I never realised he was involved with Edward Callow at the time. The entire situation seems remarkable.'

'Not really,' Rex suggested. 'Morecambe is a small town. It's not unusual for people like that to gravitate together. Some people in your life stand out more than others. It's just the way these things work.'

'Whatever happens today, Rex, I hope you can prove

your innocence. I'm sorry that things went so badly for you. Let's get these videos and any other evidence we can lay our hands on and put all this behind us. We both have our families to think of. We're almost there now; are you ready?'

Charlotte had stopped at the end of a side road. Across from them was Edward Callow's street, the houses large and imposing in the darkness. It seemed remarkable that she and Nigel Davies had only been there twelve or so hours previously. It felt as if a week had passed since then.

'We should enter the property from behind his garage; it's more secluded there. Watch out for security lights, too. We don't want to raise any alarms. We'll walk on the far side of the road. If any cars come, jump into the bushes. Okay?'

'You sound like you've done this before,' Rex observed.

'More times in the past year than a woman of my age should ever do,' Charlotte said.

She led the way. Rex was right; before they'd moved back to Morecambe, she never would have imagined doing the things she'd done. She was prepared to do much worse, if it meant that Lucia was returned safely to her.

Cautiously, they walked along the far side of the road towards Edward's house, keeping tightly tucked in against the hedges and fences. Everything was quiet, with the rich folk who lived along Edward's road safely tucked up in their beds.

'That's his garage there,' Charlotte whispered, pointing. 'We can push through that gap between the hedge and the fence. It'll give us good cover. Ready?'

Rex nodded. Charlotte led the way, pressing against the neighbour's fence and forcing her way through the hedge. It was tight, but not impossible.

'Come on,' she urged Rex.

She could see the top of Rex's head above the hedge. Within a few moments, he'd pushed himself through, albeit with a little more difficulty. She hadn't taken much time to consider Rex's age, but now she thought about it, he would have to be early to mid sixties. Perhaps they were both too long in the tooth for this. Despite a diet of prison food, Rex had still managed to get a large stomach, and that had created the problem.

'There's a security light at the back of the garage,' Charlotte warned him. 'We need to make our way past that tree and then circle back round to the house.'

'Well, there are plenty of lights on,' Rex observed. 'So somebody's at home. Any idea how to break in?'

'Let's get a measure of what we're dealing with first. If Edward is on his own, I'm bursting in there right now and threatening him with that hammer.'

She watched as Rex's hand moved to his back pocket to ensure the hammer was still there. It had better be; it was the only weapon they had. It had better be.

They passed the large willow tree growing behind the garage and headed for the back of the garden to get a better view.

'Look at the size of this place,' Rex said. 'These houses must cost a fortune. There's even a small paddock at the back. Edward Callow has to be rolling in cash.'

'Look, there's a security light above both of those patio doors, but nothing on the far side. If we approach from there, we'll be able to get a look through the windows.'

Rex followed Charlotte's lead, working along the side of the garden towards the far corner of the house.

'What kind of range do those security lights have?' Charlotte asked. 'If we're underneath them, will we trigger them?'

'They detect things in front of them, so if we keep tight to the wall, we should be fine.'

'Okay, here we go. If anybody spots us, let's separate and get out however we can. I'll meet you back at the boarded-up shop if that happens. And if they catch one of us, we call the police, right?'

'Right,' Rex agreed.

One step at a time, fearful of setting off the security lights, Charlotte moved along the wall of the house. The first window was no use. The light was off. She pressed on, with Rex close behind.

Then she heard voices, all of them male. They sounded on edge, except for Edward Callow, who was using the same clipped, controlled tone as when he'd cursed her and Nigel Davies the day before. She reached the patio doors, realising a light was on inside, and peered round the side of the frame.

Charlotte held up her hand to ask Rex to stay still. They were underneath a security lamp, but as Rex had suggested, it hadn't lit up.

Taking great care, Charlotte edged along, trying to work out what was going on inside the room. There were four of them in there; Edward Callow and the two men that had been chasing her and Will at the hospital. She could see them across the room without revealing her presence outside on the patio. With them was the man with the purple Mohican, his hand bandaged in a blood-stained dressing. Next to him, a gun was lying on Edward's kitchen worktop.

CHAPTER TWENTY-THREE

Morecambe - Present Day

Charlotte tensed the moment she saw him. This was the man who'd been with Lucia only hours earlier, the same man who'd drawn a knife on Will. One or more of those men had also attacked Will in their guest house.

And there was Edward Callow, presiding over it all, looking like he was glowing with health. He'd fallen out of his car in front of the Midland Hotel only a matter of hours previously, before his charity event had even begun properly. However he'd managed to pull off that trick, there was no doubt in Charlotte's mind that it was an act, to draw attention away from himself after the deaths of his colleagues.

She pulled back from the patio window and turned to Rex.

'All four of them are in there,' she whispered. 'There's a gun on the worktop. These guys mean business.'

'We could get them for possession of a gun if we called in the police now,' Rex suggested.

'They'd conceal it. And besides, DCI Summers would only send officers in if they fired it. I think she's scared of the fallout if she takes a wrong step with Callow, and I can't blame her. You should have heard how he threatened the young PC who was stationed on his doorstep when we visited him on Saturday morning; who knows what would happen to someone as senior as DCI Summers if she made a wrong move with him? It's all water off a duck's back to these guys. They seem to be able to operate below the radar of the police... Oh, Jesus!'

Charlotte shrieked as she realised what she'd done. As she was whispering to Rex, she'd caught sight of two glowing eyes in a nearby flower bed, and it had made her jump, activating the security light. Now she could see it was a cat, but its eyes had looked terrifying as they caught the light from the kitchen.

'Shit, we need to hide,' Rex said. 'Split up, make it harder for them to spot us. Go!'

Amid the urgent activity from inside the house, Charlotte watched Rex scuttle along the wall of the house and into a dark patch of the garden. She had only just reached the end of the house by the time she heard the key in the lock of the patio door. She could feel her heart pounding furiously.

She scanned her immediate area for a place to hide, realising she'd have to commit quickly now that the patio door was opening. There was a shed beyond the house, bordering part of the neighbour's fence, with a gap where she could conceal herself. From that position, she could get a view of the men.

'It's only a bloody cat,' she heard the man with the grav-

elly voice say as he stood on the patio with his mate. The
man with the Mohican was standing in the doorway, the
gun in his hand.

'Shall I shoot it?' he said.

Charlotte watched as Edward Callow walked up
behind him and took the weapon.

'I think you've had your fair share of trouble tonight,
don't you?' Edward said, calm and controlled. The man
with the Mohican didn't challenge him, but stepped out on
to the patio and joined the other two men in surveying the
garden. They spread out along the full width of the paved
area, triggering more sensors. Everything, from the house to
the fencing along the paddock, was now bathed in a muted
light.

Edward walked towards the garden.

'I want you to make sure it was a cat,' he said. 'Check
the whole garden, including the front of the house. We can't
afford any cock-ups tonight of all nights. It was difficult
enough to get the cops off my back, we need to make the
most of it and get the job done.'

While the men fanned out across the lawn, Charlotte
moved to the back of the shed, giving her a better view as
they moved deeper into the grounds. There was a movement by a cluster of shrubs. It was Rex. He was concealed
for now, but it wouldn't take them long to find him. So far,
Edward had stayed at the end of the patio, but as he
watched his companions, he stepped further out on to the
grass. He still had the gun in his hand.

Until tonight, Charlotte had never seen a handgun. The
closest she'd ever been to a weapon was her father's air rifle
and cousin's air pistol.

The man with the terrible voice was getting too close to
Rex. She had to catch Rex's attention and get him to force

his way into the cluster of shrubs. But he kept on circling the shrubs. It was only a matter of time before they spotted him.

Charlotte waved her hands in an attempt to catch his attention, then panicked as a shadow fell to the side of the shed, making her dart back into the gap. Edward Callow came around the side. Damn it, she'd been careless and lost track of his movements. Hiding inside the gap between the shed and the fence, every breath, every heartbeat felt loud enough to give her away. She stayed still and listened; where was he?

There was a brief knock at the back of the shed, enough to make her move to the front. It sounded like Edward had tapped the gun against the back panel of the shed as he was passing; it was enough to identify where he was.

Charlotte waited and watched. The moment she saw Edward's hand, she moved round to the front door of the shed. A cough helped her to work out he was diagonally opposite her. She listened, trying to get a sense of which way he was moving. Would he walk through the gap, as she had done, or check it was clear and head back into the garden?

She had to take a chance, peering along the gap between the shed and the fence. He wasn't there. As she ducked back, his footsteps came back, near the shed door. They were centimetres away from each other. The shed door creaked open. Charlotte dared not move. If he checked the gap again, he'd find her.

Slowly, he closed the door, as if he sensed she was there.

'There's something here!' came a voice from the other side of the garden. She heard Edward close the shed door and move away.

Charlotte began to breathe again. She moved to the far

end of the gap to see where they were gathering. They were near the shrubs. Rex must be terrified, waiting there, expecting to be discovered. There was nothing she could do for him; they'd agreed to take care of themselves. Even if they did find Rex, there was no way they'd shoot him in Edward Callow's garden; the neighbours would soon report it.

Charlotte was confident in Edward's ability to think things through. If they caught Rex, he'd be fine for a time, at least long enough for her to get the evidence she'd needed to get DCI Summers' full and undivided attention. It seemed like a plan.

Not daring to take her eyes off the garden, Charlotte moved around the back of the shed, towards the far corner of the house. Making sure that the men were occupied ahead of her, she scuttled along the wall of the house and up to the patio door, which was now wide open. The security light was still on, so she could get there without drawing attention to herself. She made one last check then stepped through the open doors and into the kitchen. As she did so, she heard a voice.

'Got you! Now step out where we can get a good look at you.'

CHAPTER TWENTY-FOUR

Morecambe - 2006

Edward had heard that the woman often went for a drink in The Battery on a Friday evening, so he made sure he was ready for her when she turned up. Unaccustomed to speaking to women in a flirtatious way, he was nervous at the prospect of striking up a casual conversation with her. But he had to find out what this woman knew.

As the newly elected local MP for the area, Edward's face was becoming much better known. It was an element of the job he struggled with; not so much fame, but notoriety. People would often recognise him on the street and start talking to him about matters which were not his direct responsibility as an MP. Usually, it related to bin collections, road repairs and street cleaning. He'd humour them and point them in the right direction to whichever department in the local council could deal with their issue. He found it easy to talk to people when they were discussing business. His problem came when it was conversational. Edward Callow was not a man for casual chit-chat.

He'd decided that in his role as a man of the people, he'd be best drinking a pint of beer that night. He generally preferred soft drinks; he'd never been drunk in his life and he disliked the lack of control that alcohol brought about. However, he was counting on its relaxing effect when he spoke to Jenna Phillips that evening.

Harvey Turnbull had proposed an audacious plan. Edward decided, on balance, that a less drastic method might be more appropriate. This was Jenna's chance to come clean and save herself a lot of grief. If she wouldn't play ball, they'd do it Harvey's way. Edward always preferred the civilised approach if it was open to them. If not, Mason Jones was on standby.

Harvey Turnbull's men had been following Jenna for several days. They'd tracked her movements, her contacts and her behaviour. Bob Moseley's report had been succinct and to the point. Edward had received a full briefing.

'She's a bit of a sad old slapper. Lives in a two-bedroom bedsit in the West End. Shares it with her daughter, who's sixteen or seventeen years of age. Used to be in teaching, left her job after a scandal. Now works part-time in a corner shop. Doesn't seem close to her daughter; you don't see them together. Goes to The Battery every Friday night and often leaves with a different man. As I said, a sad old slapper.'

Edward knew about the daughter already. She was the leverage if Jenna wasn't talkative that night.

He sat at the bar, taking occasional sips of his pint, and acknowledging the infrequent greetings from fellow drinkers who were more interested in their Friday night boozing than in politics. He was grateful for that. His single mission that night was not to get closer to his constituents but to strike up a conversation with one in particular.

Bob Moseley's information was correct; Jenna entered the bar a little after half-past seven. The Battery was busy for that time of night. A group of middle-aged men had commandeered the pool table and there was a friendly game of darts going on at the far side of the room. There was a good mix of people there, some eating meals and others meeting with friends for an end of week drink.

Several locals acknowledged Jenna, but she wasn't meeting anyone in particular. She pulled up a chair further along the bar, near a charity box that was chained to the counter, as Bob Moseley had said she would.

She ordered a Babycham. The barman was preparing it before the words had left her mouth. Edward observed her without being creepy, pretending to be engrossed in the game of darts that was getting boisterous elsewhere in the bar.

It pained Edward to be judgemental, but Jenna looked like she'd seen better days. Her clothing was cheap, probably from one of the local markets, and her make-up was overdone. She'd made a cursory effort to spruce herself up for a Friday night, but that only amounted to taking care of the basics. She looked sad, as if her spirit had been crushed.

Edward simply observed these things. He wasn't the slightest bit concerned as to why Jenna was in that situation. He considered how he could engage her in conversation without suggesting it was a romantic approach, which would horrify him.

'Do you have cheese and onion crisps?' he asked the barman. He knew already that the answer to that question was yes. Handing over a note and receiving a handful of change, he placed the small coins into the charity box. Jenna looked at him.

'This seems like a good cause to support. Do you know anything about them?' he asked.

'Yes, they do good work in this area. Don't I know you? Are you a celebrity?'

Edward smiled. That was helpful; she'd seen his picture somewhere. It brought it on to more comfortable ground, a casual conversation between a new MP and a constituent.

'I'm the town's new MP. I haven't been in the post that long, so I'm amazed that you even recognised me. I must be doing something right.'

'Ah, yes. You're the guy who built the new school. I'm pleased you did; my daughter goes there now, and it's a lovely building, much better than the old place. What are you doing here drinking in this place on a Friday night?'

'I try to get out every now and again. It's a good opportunity to talk to my constituents and find out what's on their minds. I won't stay long. It gets rather wild when the drinks are flowing. But it's useful for me to get a feel for what's bothering people in the town.'

'Sounds fair enough,' Jenna replied.

'Can I get you a drink?' Edward chanced. 'The British government is buying. I'd love to ask your opinion on something if you have a minute.'

'Yes, why not? This is better than the normal conversation I get in here on a Friday night. I'll have a glass of dry white wine, please.'

Edward placed the order and moved his chair and drink closer to Jenna. He'd already seen the pace at which she drank the Babycham. He suspected the wine wouldn't last long.

'So you have a daughter at the school? Have you lived in the area long?'

Edward continued asking questions that remained on safe territory. As he talked to her about her former work in education, her thoughts on the regeneration activity in the resort and what her daughter's plans were after leaving school, he watched her gulp down two glasses of wine. As the wine was drunk, her tongue became looser, and there was a slight slurring to her words.

This was right where he wanted her: drunk enough to relax and maintain a conversation, but not so drunk that she would start speaking nonsense. It occurred to him for one moment that had he been predatory, this process would have been simple. Jenna was vulnerable, poor and—it seemed—in desperate need of company. He delivered his killer question.

'So, did you ever work in the arcades or at the old amusement park during the summer holidays? Half of Morecambe seems to have done that while they were students.'

'No, I never did that. I only worked one summer, because they used to pay our rent and social security in those days. My daughter can't believe it when I tell her that now. But I worked that first summer, at the Sandy Beaches Holiday Camp.'

'Oh, you worked there, did you?' Edward smiled. No wonder women got themselves into such trouble on nights out. He was finding this easier than a business transaction.

'Yes, it was a right tip. It closed a long time ago now. Have they knocked it down yet?'

'It's an intriguing site. I've always had an interest in building there myself. The plot of land would be much better suited to quality housing, in my opinion.'

Jenna seemed bored by the sudden turn in the conversation to business matters, and picked up her glass, sipping the final drops of wine.

'Can I get you another one?' Edward asked. 'I won't join you, I have to leave in a few minutes, but what you've told me is very interesting, thank you.'

He wanted to assure her that this was not a flirtation; she needed to see him as an MP, not a Friday night prospect.

The third glass of white wine arrived. It was time to go in for the kill.

'I met a gentleman who worked there once, many years ago. In this pub, as it happens. I was meeting with a friend, and there were a few rowdy students. We were sitting over there, actually. And he was propping up the bar to your right. These students started throwing beer mats, and it was annoying me and my friend. He stepped in and sorted them out for us. He worked in bars at the holiday camp, he told me afterwards. That'll be where he got his training to deal with those students. That must have been about the same time you were there, mid-nineteen-eighties?'

Edward noticed how Jenna stiffened. He'd have to push a little harder to get the information he wanted.

'I can't remember his name. Craven, I think it was. Brian, Bruce, Bryce? Something like that. Did you know him?

Jenna finished her sip of wine and placed the wine glass on the bar.

'I know your game,' she said to him, sounding sober. 'And you can get stuffed!'

She placed a twenty-pound note on the bar.

'And you can stick your drinks!'

She left the pub, leaving Edward wondering if anyone

had observed what just happened. The pub was noisier, and it seemed to have passed without drawing attention.

He picked up the twenty-pound note and pushed it into the slot of the charity box. Then he took out his mobile phone and keyed in a number.

'Mason? It's Edward.'

'Hi Edward, so?'

'We're on. Do it. Next week, as we discussed. Let's see what this woman knows about Bruce Craven.'

CHAPTER TWENTY-FIVE

Morecambe - Present Day

Charlotte stopped dead in Edward's doorway. There was nobody inside the house, so she turned around. To her relief, she realised she hadn't been seen; it must be Rex they were talking to. She took cover in the doorway, feeling much safer within the confines of the house.

The floodlight above the patio windows from the kitchen reached far into the garden. She strained her eyes to work out what was going on.

She could make out Edward Callow's shape, and there were two men—no, three men—the silhouette of that Mohican hairstyle was distinctive, even from a distance. They'd found Rex Emery.

Her instinct was to shout or help him, but that wasn't an option. They'd both understood they were jumping into the deep end. Rex needed Edward Callow to be taken care of as much as she did. If there was one thing about men like

Edward, it was that he wouldn't be so foolish as to harm Rex on his own property. That bought her valuable time.

She surveyed the kitchen. It oozed wealth and opulence; the worktop was natural granite, and the cupboards looked handmade from quality wood. There were two vases packed with fresh flowers, numerous wines tidily stored in racks and a bowl of mixed, fresh fruit in the middle of the table. Charlotte thought of their own fruit bowl which looked abandoned and neglected; the last time she'd seen it, it had contained a shrivelled orange and a black banana.

Her instinct was to take her shoes off, careful not to tread mud into the cream white carpet beyond the kitchen.

'He doesn't have kids,' she thought to herself. In Charlotte's experience, cream carpets were made only for the childless and people capable of walking from one end of a room to the other holding a hot drink without spilling a drop. The rest of the population was excluded from the experience.

She did remove her shoes, but not to preserve Edward's carpet. Now she was inside the house, she had every intention of staying until she found something—anything—which would give DCI Summers immediate cause to start investigating him.

She walked from the kitchen into a vast hall. She'd caught a glimpse of it the day before when she'd door stepped Edward, alongside Nigel Davies. Nigel would come if he needed her, now that Will was out of action. She still had a friend she could rely on if she needed someone to help her.

As she walked towards the wide staircase, still cream carpeted and with a heavy, wooden, hand-carved railing, she peeked into the lounge. It was massive, with four white, leather sofas circling the biggest television set she had ever seen. There was an expensive-looking stereo in the corner, its speakers modern, minimalist and hi-tech. She almost burst out laughing at the small, ornate chandelier that lit the room, but the roaring log fire made her long for the freedom to curl up on the rug in front of it and fall asleep there.

Charlotte heard a noise, as if someone was pressing a hand against the front door; somebody must be coming in. She ran up the stairs as fast as she could, thankful that they didn't creak.

Edward Callow didn't have to concern himself with electricity bills either. Almost every light in the house was switched on. There were six bedrooms, and two shared bathrooms upstairs.

She listened as the door opened downstairs. It sounded like one person; they walked into the kitchen, collected something and went outside again. It was probably just one of the men forgetting a phone or coming into the house to collect something. She relaxed again, as much as she could, bearing in mind her present situation.

Charlotte couldn't resist looking inside their open doors to see how this man lived. All the rooms had fresh flowers and an en suite bathroom. It was more like a hotel, and a nice one at that. Every inch screamed class and quality, but it was the residence of a man who had no family. Its neatness suggested a daily cleaner and a complete absence of children or animals.

There was one room at the far end of the landing which she hadn't investigated yet. Feeling much safer now the house was empty, she headed for it and opened the door. It was Edward's office. She'd hit the jackpot. The main light was switched off, but a desktop lamp served to illuminate the area sufficiently well. An entire wall was taken up by books. Charlotte scanned the titles, realising that they were all non-fiction publications. There wasn't a single work of fiction in his entire collection.

The desk was of oak, as she might have expected, and immaculately tidy. Two Apple PC screens dominated the space and a lean, metallic keyboard lay on the desk. Then she spotted something discordant, bearing in mind the amount of money that had been lavished on every inch of this property. It was a plastic supermarket bag, abandoned in the far corner.

Charlotte placed her shoes inside the door and walked over to the bag. She checked the wooden blinds to make sure that she couldn't be seen from outside. They were almost fully closed, but there was enough of a gap for her to peer through and see the drive outside.

The external lighting was off at the front of the house, but if she strained her eyes, she could just about see what was going on. They were taking Rex Emery to the garage, which ran at right angles to the front of the house, allowing her a clear view inside from her vantage point of the upstairs window. Two cars were parked next to Edward's on the driveway.

Rex's mouth was covered with tape or a gag of some sort and his arms and legs were bound securely. Thankfully he didn't look hurt, which made her feel less treacherous about leaving him on his own. She wouldn't be much help against those men.

Charlotte could almost make out the number plate on one of the cars. She returned to Edward's desk and picked a piece of paper out of the bin. A fountain pen had been placed neatly to the side of the computer keyboard. It was heavy in the hand, a make she didn't recognise. She took a best guess at the plate details and wrote them down.

Would there be something in the plastic bag that would allow her to tip off the police about Rex? She struck gold straight away; it was packed with the videos from the shop. If she had to, she'd send one to every TV and radio station in the north of England.

She reached into her pocket for her phone and dialled Nigel Davies. It was still holding a charge, but only just.

It rang several times before he picked up. That was understandable, considering it was half-past three in the morning.

'Nigel, it's Charlotte,'

'Have they found Lucia?' he asked in a sleepy voice.

'No, but I need you to listen to me, Nigel. You might have to make excuses to that patient wife of yours.'

'Don't worry. I was dozing in the sitting room. I half expected a call. It's been a crazy day. Where are you?'

'I'm in Edward Callow's study—'

'That's insane, Charlotte. Please tell me you haven't broken in?'

'No, not really. The door was wide open. Look, I need your help. I want you to pick up a bag of videos and put them somewhere safe, where they won't be found. Will you do that for me?'

'Where will you leave them?'

As Nigel was speaking, a plain, brown envelope caught Charlotte's eye, lying on top of a row of books on one of the bookshelves. It seemed unusual for Edward to leave something like that.

'Remember when we were here, and you threw stones at Edward's roof? Go to the far end of Edward's garage and squeeze through the gap between the hedge and the fence.'

'You realise you're playing with fire, Charlotte?'

She ignored him and carried on, perching her phone

between her chin and her shoulder so she could pick up the brown envelope.

'Edward has motion sensor lights surrounding the house, so stay wide. Work your way around the garden, along the fencing that borders his paddock, then work your way back towards the house, but no further than the shed. I'm leaving a plastic bag for you there, in the gap between the shed and the fence. It looks like a charity bag packed with rubbish, but it's not. The videos in that bag can sully several reputations in this town.'

'I'll do it, but please be safe.'

'I've got to go, I don't have much battery left. I'll let you know as soon as there's anything else.'

Charlotte ended the call and put the phone back in her pocket, frustrated that she'd forgotten to pass on the number plate details. She decided not to call back, she could text it to Nigel later when she was in a less vulnerable situation.

Then she opened the brown envelope and pulled out three A4-sized photographs, stunned by what she saw. Each of the photos had been taken from a distance, as if from a surveillance operation.

But it was the subjects of the images which shocked her the most. Each photograph showed George and Isla walking along the promenade with Una. Which meant that whatever Isla had told her was likely to have been a pack of lies. It looked like she was in this up to her neck.

CHAPTER TWENTY-SIX

Morecambe - Present Day

Charlotte felt a surge of rage, frustration and disappointment, remembering the time she'd asked Isla about this. She'd been tight-lipped and evasive, as if trying to hide something from them. But what?

The thought of Isla being a criminal mastermind was preposterous. But she did know these men. She'd encountered them at The Lakes View Guest House. And yet she'd claimed not to remember Rex Emery.

Charlotte put the photographs back into the envelope and placed it in the plastic bag with the videos. Would it be enough evidence for DCI Summers? Probably not, but it was a start. She walked around the room, examining each bookshelf to see if anything else had been left there. Next, she tried the three drawers in Edward's desk. They were locked, of course.

She glanced out of the window again. The man with the gravelly voice had clicked a remote unit, and the garage door was closing behind them. Rex was being shut inside with the men. That wasn't good. The only option was to place the plastic bag for Nigel to pick up, then alert the police to save Rex from whatever they had planned for him. Didn't Edward have a landline? There were no cables anywhere.

Charlotte picked up the plastic bag along with her shoes and made her way down the stairs, listening and watching the front door like a hawk. If somebody walked in now, they'd catch her. At the bottom, she hurried towards the kitchen, placed the bag on the kitchen floor and leaned against the door frame to put on her shoes. As she did so, Edward Callow walked in from the lounge.

She hid her shoes behind the door then darted towards the central island in the kitchen for cover. Edward was humming to himself as he walked to the coffee machine at the far wall. The fridge was right behind her. If Edward went for the milk or cream, he'd be heading her way.

She tried to figure out a plan of attack.

There were kitchen knives behind her. If he discovered her, she could grab one of those. Her own knives at home were blunt, but she was willing to bet that Edward's would be as sharp as a gladiator's sword. It would all be useless in any case; Edward had a gun. A kitchen knife would be no match. Depending on whether he veered to the left or right of the island, if she was fast, she could avoid him by shuffling to the opposite side. But she had to do something with the bag of videos.

At each corner of the central island in the kitchen was a storage shelf, occupied with kitchen gadgets on the right-hand side but empty on the other side. The sounds of the coffee machine gurgling gave her sufficient cover to place the bag into the storage area. There were no other options.

Besides, Edward was now heading for the fridge, as she'd anticipated.

Charlotte shuffled to the right-hand side, uncomfortable squatting but afraid to stretch out, in case he saw her.

For a few seconds, she wasn't sure what he was doing other than putting milk in his coffee. Everything went quiet. Then he walked across and pulled out a stool on the far side of the island. He was drinking his coffee less than a metre away from her.

Charlotte's legs were in cramp; she'd be incapable of making her escape if she needed to run for it. Then a phone began to ring in another room, a mobile phone rather than a landline. It looked like Edward had opted for a wireless system around his house.

He got off his chair and walked out of the kitchen. Charlotte could see one of her shoes poking out from behind the door. She held her breath as he walked past it, then stood up, hobbling as the blood began to flow back into her legs. As fast as she could, she retrieved her shoes, putting them in the plastic bag and made for the patio door, which was now closed.

Edward was speaking on the phone.

'Yes, go ahead. But make sure the neighbours don't see or hear anything. We need to make sure we have every copy of those videos.'

If the patio door was locked, he'd walk straight in on her. Charlotte shut her eyes as she pushed the handle. Thank God it opened. She went into the garden and turned to close the door, just as Edward walked back into the kitchen. If he'd looked up from his phone, he would have seen her.

Charlotte retraced her steps along the side of the house and left the bag at the far end of the shed for Nigel. Once she'd put on her shoes, she made her way around the perimeter of the garden, back towards the garage.

Concealed behind a well-grown shrub, Charlotte took her phone out of her pocket in the hope that it might muster enough charge to phone or text Nigel Davies. Realising it was almost dead, she was about to move on when her foot stood on a hard object. As she reached down, her fingers touched something heavy and cold. It was the end of a hammer.

It was Rex's hammer. He must have dropped it in the scuffle. She picked it up and slid the handle into her back pocket together with her phone. The hammer felt cumbersome, but it might come in handy.

As she neared the garage, she noticed that the side facing the garden didn't have a security light. There was a small window built into that wall too.

Slowly, she moved towards the window, avoiding the sensors. She couldn't abandon Rex, not after he'd helped her. If they were hurting him, she'd find a way of raising the alarm.

Taking great care to make sure she didn't reveal herself to the three men, Charlotte looked inside the garage. It was big enough for four or five cars, but there was only a single sports car parked in there, plus a substantial motorcycle and garden equipment.

Rex Emery was motionless in the chair, still restrained. The man with the Mohican was looking on, smirking, enjoying every minute of what the other two men were doing to Rex.

The man with the gravelly voice struck Rex across the chin with a confident punch, and Rex's head dropped, limp and still. He'd taken enough punishment and had passed out from the beating.

CHAPTER TWENTY-SEVEN

Morecambe - 2006

'Do we have to have this bloody photo taken?' Harvey Turnbull complained. 'We're being paraded like rabbits at a pet show. They'll rib me mercilessly about this back at the station.'

'Just suck it up and smile for the camera,' Edward muttered. He'd never particularly taken to Harvey Turnbull at a personal level, primarily because at their first encounter the police officer had held all the cards. However, his two thugs had been effective, discreet and cheap to keep on the payroll. But now, he was having second thoughts about Harvey. Once this issue with the woman was taken care of, he had a plan to deal with him.

'This is our alibi,' Edward said in a low voice, spotting that Rex Emery was in the room. Emery was another man he didn't like. He was too servile for Edward's tastes, and not strong enough. However, like Turnbull's thugs, Rex was reliable and cheap. He was also going to be in a lot deeper with Edward after that day's business was concluded.

'With us all gathered like this and smiling for the camera, there's no doubt whatsoever of our whereabouts at this moment in time. Mason has sorted everything out with the girl, so all you have to do is to visit the Phillips woman and put the squeeze on her. It'll make a change for you to earn your money for once. Once you've delivered this little job, we'll discuss that increase in earnings you wanted.'

Harvey looked as if he wanted to release a tirade of abuse, but the lure of the extra cash appeared to be enough for him to keep his mouth shut. Edward turned away and grinned to himself; he found these men so predictable. It was like a game of cat and mouse in which he was the cat who always caught the mouse.

Rory Higson arrived along with Mason and Barry, who looked like they'd run into him whilst parking up cars at the front of the guest house.

'Everything in hand, Mason?' Edward asked, by way of a greeting.

Mason nodded and carried on his conversation with Barry. The two men had hit it off over the years; an author and a head teacher didn't seem to be the most obvious of bedfellows, yet their shared interests tended not to be in business matters.

Fred Walker was last to arrive.

'Sorry everyone, couldn't get the Bentley parked,' he announced, out of breath and red-faced. Fred insisted on driving the biggest car available, equating it with prestige and success.

Edward tried to maintain his cool while Rory Higson staged the photograph, but his patience was wearing thin. He was also on edge about the girl; they were playing with fire, but he had to be sure that Bruce Craven was not coming back to bite them. The investigation by the Newcastle police was not going away, regardless of Harvey Turnbull's best efforts; it was beginning to weigh on Edward's mind.

He was gasping for a coffee, and Rex Emery was nowhere to be seen. Edward looked around. The coffee machine was spluttering away, but still, there was no hot drink in front of him. He laid into Rex when he appeared in the lounge; it was not his normal style, but it served another purpose for Edward other than just laying his hands on a drink. He was softening Rex up for what was coming afterwards.

Rory Higson took an age to set up the shot, moving them around the table as he tried to compensate for Fred Walker's huge frame. Edward cringed as he watched Harvey Turnbull deliberately knock his drink off the table as the lady who was serving it placed it at his side. This was the problem with Harvey; he was a spiteful bully, accustomed to holding all the cards.

Edward reflected for a moment; was what he was doing to Rex Emery any different to what Harvey was doing? He believed it was. Where Harvey picked on innocent victims —this Isla woman was of no interest to anybody and formed no part of any business strategy—Rex Emery was about to become a key player and a fall guy. With Rex, it was business, whereas with Isla, Harvey was humiliating a woman because he could, because he held power over her.

At last, the photo session was finished. More importantly, Edward had got that coffee at last, and he was calmer, ready for his conversation with Rex Emery.

Rory Higson signified everything that Edward hated about the town; he was a small thinker, happy with his crappy job on the paper and aspiring to nothing more than that. It was a mindset that Edward couldn't understand. Rory must spend his life photographing groups with giant cardboard cheques and businesspeople shaking hands over some deal or other. Why hadn't it driven Rory crazy? Edward often wondered what divided men like him and men like Rory Higson. Was it their complete lack of aspiration and ambition?

Rory was done at long last, muttering a lot of nonsense about the group photograph making history. Edward suspected that after the picture appeared in that week's paper, it would most likely end up as lining for cat litter trays soon afterwards, never looked at again. That was fine by him. It had given them the alibi they needed to deflect attention. He looked at his watch; they would have the girl by now.

Edward had warned Rex that he wanted to talk to him before Rory's farewell, so as the room began to clear, he gave the nod to indicate that he was ready to talk.

'My apologies once again that the coffee wasn't ready. We had the last of the paying guests to see to, and we were rushed—'

Edward held his hand up; he didn't give a damn.

'Is the place empty now?' he asked.

'My wife and daughter are still in our living quarters; all the guests have either checked out or have gone off for the day.'

Bob Moseley walked into the lounge, dead on time. He'd taken a seat, waiting for Edward to acknowledge him when he was ready.

'I'm sorry sir, we're not open—'

Rex began to speak, but Edward interrupted.

'He's with me.'

Rex looked at Bob, uncertain, but he didn't say anything more.

'Is there a back door?' Edward asked. It was a rhetorical question.

'Yes, why?'

'Leave it ajar please. Bob needs to bring something in the back.'

'But—'

Rex began to protest but thought better of it and went off to open the door.

'Wait until I confirm the room,' he said to Bob, then moved into the hall to wait for Rex at the bottom of the staircase.

'I want to hire one of the rooms,' Edward began as Rex returned from the back of the guest house. 'I'll pay you four times as much as a guest would pay. In cash, so it doesn't have to go through the books. I want to rent the room for one month. During that month, you will never enter the room, and you will never go in to change the linen or clean it. Understood?'

Edward noticed how each time he spoke, Rex looked like he was about to protest, then backed down. This was what the softening up was about; it trained men like Rex to understand the only option was to comply.

'May I ask what you'll be using it for?' Rex asked.

'Business,' Edward replied. 'The man who's waiting in the lounge at the moment will be your guest. You'll see him from time to time. But stay out of that room, it's being used for the business on a temporary basis.'

Although he was reluctant to do it, Edward could see the deal would have to be cemented with a threat to Rex's family. He'd get Bob to do that later. It would focus Rex's mind and make him understand he was being given instructions, not being asked for permission.

'I'd like you to show me what rooms you have available, so I can select the best one.'

'The only room that's free at the moment is the guest room at the top of the stairs. People complain about the seagulls being so close on the roof, so we always save it until last. Do you want to take a look?'

Edward moved his arm, inviting Rex to show him the way. Bob Moseley joined them in the corridor.

'Follow us, Bob. This will be your room.'

They walked up the stairs to the fourth floor of the guest house, and Rex opened the bedroom door. Guest house rooms all looked the same to Edward, but he could tell that this room was perfect. It was separated from the adjacent rooms by a bathroom, the seagulls were making a racket on the roof overhead, and there was a small door leading to a roof space. There was also a sink in the room itself; it was perfect for what they had in mind.

'Everything alright for you, Bob?' Edward asked.

He nodded.

Edward reached in his pocket, took out a plain, white envelope and handed it to Rex.

'Inside that envelope is one thousand pounds in cash. That's for room hire and a midday meal. I want you and your family to get lost for the next hour while we move in some essential business equipment. Get that wife of yours and your daughter and take a walk. Don't come back before one o'clock.'

'But what if a guest needs to get in?' Rex asked.

'Rex, it's a nice day outside. Take a walk, spend a bit of money, treat your family. You've been working hard. You all deserve a break.'

Edward could see the sum of money was pitched right. Rex's eyes had lit up as he touched the notes, his greed getting the better of him.

As Rex headed down the stairs to the family quarters, Edward followed close behind, less concerned now that the early stages of the plan had played out so well. As he reached the bottom step, he noticed the woman Harvey had been bullying—Isla whatever her name was—wandering into the kitchen. Edward noted he'd have to watch out for her. She moved about the place like a family member, with access everywhere. He'd have to make sure she didn't see anything that she shouldn't.

CHAPTER TWENTY-EIGHT

Morecambe - Present Day

Charlotte flinched as she peered through the garage window. She was grateful for the shadow cast by Edward's house at the side of the garage, the darkness prevented her from being too exposed. She'd been spared from violence for most of her life, but on the few occasions she'd encountered it, she had found it terrifying. It didn't matter whether it was underhand and hidden, as with Bruce Craven at first, or explosive and aggressive, like the time Bruce had confronted them when they got off the bus at Sandy Beaches Holiday Camp; it always shocked her.

In Charlotte's world, it was unconscionable that one person would want to do that to another. She'd never even smacked her own children. Yet there she was, her hand on the top of the hammer in her pocket, ready at a moment's notice to crack one of those men on the head, if it would alleviate Rex Emery's pain. George had got it right after they'd rescued Lucia from Pat and Jenna; *sometimes good people have to do bad things.*

She'd lost count of how many times she'd run all of this through her head now. She and Will were victims. They hadn't invited any of this into their lives. But she could never shake off the sense that they'd brought it all on themselves. If they'd told the truth after that night, would any of this have happened?

At one time, after Jenna's deception had been revealed, Charlotte might have opted for taking the honest approach. She and Will should have confessed to the holiday camp bosses what had happened that night with Bruce. The police would have got involved, Jenna might have been revealed as Bruce's killer, and it would have all blown over for them. But they didn't know about Jenna at the time, nor George come to that. They'd made their decisions based on fear; they'd only been kids, after all.

Charlotte thought about her own daughter. Lucia's judgement was often poor, to say the least. At that age, it was all about self-preservation. Thinking back to her own terror during Bruce's attack, she still believed she'd made the right decision. They'd thought Bruce was gone, both figuring they'd been mistaken about the level of harm they'd inflicted upon him. He'd had formidable strength, so they'd reckoned he must have only been stunned, knocked out cold. The gush of relief had been immense the next day, when it seemed that he'd got up and left the holiday camp.

Whichever way she looked at it, even another three decades after the situation, she still didn't think she'd do anything differently. Well, maybe one thing: she and Will should have been more honest with each other. Yet which couple would pass a true test of honesty, never mind how open they professed to be? Most people only shared what was palatable, an edited version of the reality in their head. And that's why they'd kept the terrible secret for so long.

These men would continue their cruelty, threatening, intimidating and callously wrecking lives, until a force greater than theirs stepped in to stop them.

Two of the thugs were untying Rex from the chair. There was an altercation with the man with the Mohican hairstyle. He held up his bandaged hand, as if he was being admonished for not helping more. She hoped his hand hurt like hell.

Rex was left with his hands and legs restrained and tape over his mouth, but he was no longer tied to the chair. He slumped to the ground; none of the men appeared to be concerned about that. They were moving to the front of the garage, opening up the door, reversing one of the cars in.

Emboldened by their state of distraction, Charlotte tried to attract Rex's attention through the window as he lay on the floor. She checked that she couldn't be seen from the adjacent house; lucky for her, Edward was well away from the garage, at the back of the house where the kitchen was located. Rex was struggling to force open his eyes; even from that distance, she could tell they were bruised and bloody.

The security light to her side lit up, and she was alert for a moment, fearing she'd been spotted. But it was a man on the driveway who'd triggered the sensor as he got into another car to start it. She finally attracted Rex's attention through the small side window, and he looked up towards her.

She wanted to call to him, to reassure him she would help, but it was useless. In the end, all she could do was to hold up her phone to indicate she would call the police. Charlotte hoped Rex would understand what she meant.

These thugs would get caught in the act. It would be enough for DCI Summers to pull Edward Callow in for questioning.

The man finished reversing the car into the garage, and the door was closed again. The same two-man team picked Rex up by his arms and legs and threw him into the boot of the car, closing it as soon as his head was clear.

Charlotte had a decision to make: to call the police now, or let things play out a little longer, in the hope they'd take her to Lucia. She only had a moment to make her decision; one of the men had stepped into the car and was getting ready to drive it. The other man was moving back to the garage door to open it up. The man with the Mohican was rubbing his bandaged hand, taking a back seat and watching it all play out.

She moved to the end of the garage wall and looked at the other cars on the drive. The front doors of the second plain car were open, as if the vehicle was about to be driven. At that moment, she took a chance.

Charlotte ran at the car, opened the back door just as she heard the garage door opening up, and concealed herself in the footwell at the rear of the vehicle, clicking the door shut behind her. Her heart began to pound in her chest, hardly able to believe she'd taken the most hazardous option. She checked her phone to make sure it was on silent. The battery was almost dead, less than ten percent life. She'd have to make it count now.

Above the hum of another car's engine, she could hear Edward again, talking quietly with the men to avoid attracting any attention from the neighbours. Fat chance of that, with the distance between these properties.

As somebody got into the driver's seat in front of her, she felt the backrest pushing against her side. The driver shut the door, and another man got into the passenger side. It was Edward. The ignition started, and the car began to move.

'We sail after six o'clock,' Edward said. 'If we can sort out this bloody family by morning, it'll all be sewn up.'

Charlotte pressed herself into the corner of the footwell, curling up as small as she could, scared that Edward might see her out of the corner of his eye. She was cramped and uncomfortable but wanted to see if she could record any of this conversation on her phone. Holding it into her stomach to conceal as much screen light as possible, she waited until they were at traffic lights and pressed the record button on the voice notes app.

The second man's voice sounded coarse and sore.

'What are we doing with Emery?'

'The usual,' Edward replied. 'We still have the spare container, yes?'

'Yeah, it's still there.'

'And you're certain the last of the videos is in that derelict shop along the promenade?'

'Yeah, he was a tough bugger, but he spoke in the end. We'll set it on fire, make it look like an old tramp. Nobody will find it. The rest are in the plastic bag.'

The drive wasn't long. Charlotte guessed they were in Heysham or thereabouts. There was a guard who seemed to know them, and she gathered from the conversation that the two cars had travelled together. The car came to a stop somewhere dark, away from street lighting. Charlotte remained curled up in the back, hoping the voices would die down and give her a chance to get out.

She listened, straining to work out the gist of the muffled conversations, and switched off the recording app. Only five percent battery life remained. She had to place the call soon, or they were on their own.

CHAPTER TWENTY-NINE

Morecambe - Present Day

Charlotte had never been to the port before, but she knew of its existence from the road signs. The bus that took them back to the Sandy Beaches Holiday Camp had passed the port area, though they'd never taken a proper look at it. It just wasn't on their radar as youngsters.

The cars had been parked between two rows of battered, weathered containers, some piled three units high. There was lighting around the perimeter of the area, but it was dark between the containers. It smelled damp and oily, though the pervasive and distinctive salty tang of sea water permeated the entire yard. Underfoot, it was muddy and wet.

She would have to find a hiding place fast; whatever the men were up to, they'd be back soon. But first, she needed to make Rex aware she was there, that he hadn't been abandoned. She rushed to the other car and felt in the darkness for the button to release the boot. Looking around before pressing it, she opened the boot a little and ducked down to whisper to Rex.

'Rex, it's Charlotte.'

There was a stifled mumble; his mouth was still bound. She hoped he had enough air in there.

'Rex, I'm here. I'm calling the police. I've got Edward Callow recorded, talking about what's going on. They're going to burn down the shop and destroy the video. Damn, they're coming. I've got to go, Rex. Don't worry; someone will come for you. I won't leave you.'

Charlotte pushed down the boot, waiting for the click to make sure it was closed tight before moving into a gap between two nearby containers, taking cover and peering round the side to wait for the men.

They were speaking quietly, moving as if they'd done this a thousand times before. Charlotte didn't realise her foot was in a puddle until the cold water seeped through to her shoe.

She darted behind the container and took out her phone. Three percent battery life. Dare she call while they were on the other side of the unit? She decided to text instead; but she didn't want DCI Summers there, not until she had seen her daughter for herself. If the sirens started sounding, the men would panic and might do something rash. She was there to find Lucia, that was all that mattered. DCI Summers could do what she wanted after that.

Edward had said they were sailing at six o'clock or thereabouts. That meant any time from five o'clock would be perfect for catching them in the act, whatever it was they were doing. She knew nothing about boats, ships or sailing, but had enough knowledge to understand you didn't set sail without some kind of preparation beforehand.

She began to key in a text to Nigel Davies, hoping he was following her instructions.

Promise me not to send DCI Summers before 5am. Then I'll tell you where I am.

She sent the text and checked her sound had been disabled.

Signs of movement and engine noise were coming from the cars on the other side of the container. They must be moving Rex Emery.

She waited; there was no response from Nigel.

Torn between getting a look at what was going on and checking for a response from Nigel, she waited a little longer. At last, she got a reply.

PLEASE don't do anything foolish. I promise I'll keep quiet. I'm about to pick up the bag now. N

At Heysham Port. Rex Emery here. No police until after 5am. Send ambulance then. Callow's house empty should be safe.

Charlotte pressed send, then her phone died. That was it. She'd got her message out to Nigel. He'd raise the alarm in half an hour. That's how long she had to find out what these devils were up to. That's how long she had to save her daughter.

Charlotte jumped up to place her phone on the top of the container. It took her a few tries, but at last she positioned it at the corner where it wouldn't be seen. She took note of where it was. If anything happened before the police got there, at least she had recordings of Edward, and Nigel would save the bag of videos. It wasn't much, but it was a start. There was the photograph of George and Isla too; how she wanted to speak to them and find out what Isla had been hiding all that time. It occurred to her for one moment that perhaps Edward had been watching Isla and George; but why?

She could hear a heavy engine revving up ahead now, a lorry perhaps, moving towards where the men were waiting. Charlotte checked the hammer was still in her pocket, then moved around the far side of the container so she could get a sense of what was going on. As she peered round it, the space between the containers was illuminated by the head-lights of a lorry. The doors of a nearby container were now wide open. They were carrying Rex Emery by his arms and legs towards the opening. Stopping in front of the container, they stood him up while the man with the Mohican walked towards them. He had a bin bag in his hand and a reel of tape. Without any hesitation, he forced the bag over Rex's head and began to fumble at the tape.

'I can't do it,' he said to the man with the grating voice.

'Fucking idiot, getting your hand chewed up like that by a college tutor.'

That gave Charlotte a moment of pride in what Will had done earlier.

The man took the tape, tore off a long strip, and secured it around Rex's neck. Rex was then pushed into the container and the door secured. Charlotte had seen this before; it was how they'd tried to kill Piper. She needed them to go away, so she could help Rex. How long did he have? Would he be panicking more than she was? She had to get to him.

A big man was getting out of the lorry. He began to speak in a low voice, hard to understand at first, until Charlotte realised he wasn't speaking English. It sounded Eastern European.

Edward did the talking, waving the other three men

away. They walked off, towards the gate and over to the main part of the docks as far as she could tell. Edward seemed reasonably fluent in whatever language it was they were speaking. With the other three men now walking off into the distance, Charlotte wondered if she dared risk trying to get to Rex. How long did he have? She had to help him, but what could she do without ending up the same way?

Edward had shaken hands with the man, and they were moving to the back of the lorry. This was Charlotte's chance. As they disappeared, she ran to the container where Rex was being held and fumbled with the opening mechanism, grateful that the clanging noise was masked by the lorry's engine.

At last, she was inside the container. She pulled the door closed just enough to let light in from the headlamps. The men had not looked back to catch sight of her, she'd managed to make the move undetected. Rex was thrashing around desperately on the floor. He'd managed to tear the plastic bag on the rough, wooden flooring, and although he was starved of air, at least he was alive. Charlotte ripped open the plastic bag and tore it off Rex's head. He was drenched in sweat.

'Don't call out,' she whispered as she placed her hand over the tape on his mouth and tore it off. He took deep, desperate gasps for air.

'I'll be back. I have to see what they're doing,' she said. 'Stay quiet. I promise I'll come for you.'

Charlotte checked the coast was clear before leaving the container, firmly closing the door again. She daren't leave it open; she hoped Rex would stay quiet now he knew help was coming.

She crept to the back of Rex's container, counting along three of the units before making her way to the front again to get a view of what was going on at the back of the lorry. She'd estimated correctly; she was now behind the vehicle and could see Edward and the foreign man silhouetted against the open rear door. They were speaking in whatever language it was, seemingly to somebody at the back of the lorry.

A torch beam appeared. Charlotte assumed the driver of the lorry had taken it out of his pocket. He was shouting angrily at someone inside. The beam of the torch flashed inside the rear of the vehicle.

Charlotte stood paralysed by the glimpse she'd had of their cargo. This was a refrigerated vehicle. And it was carrying human beings.

CHAPTER THIRTY

Morecambe - 2006

Edward found he was surprisingly calm about abducting sixteen-year-old school girls. At first, he'd been jittery, half-expecting Mason Jones to mess something up. But he had to hand it to the man when it came to charming teenagers; he demonstrated great skill and ability.

The intimidation of Jenna Phillips had begun, and Edward discovered he enjoyed this game. To him, victims were like pieces on a chessboard; it was merely a matter of manoeuvring your opponent's king into a checkmate situation, and you were away, the victory was yours.

Piper Phillips was being held in the loft space in Rex's guest house. The room was perfect. The girl was out of the way there, bound and gagged, and Harvey Turnbull was dealing with the police side of things. Harvey had made a pre-emptive visit to Jenna, informing her that her daughter had gone missing from the school, describing the Newcastle police investigation into Bruce Craven's whereabouts, and leaving her in no doubt about what was required from her.

As Harvey had de-briefed Edward about his visit to Jenna's bedsit, Edward had—for a moment—considered a reprieve for Harvey. But when he began pushing for more money once again, Harvey effectively shot himself in the foot. His fate was sealed. Once Jenna Phillips was dealt with, Edward would be tying up loose ends.

He'd called in at the Lakes View Guest House unannounced, thinking it was the best way to check that the arrangements for Piper's safe-keeping were being observed. It was the MPs' summer recess, which gave him plenty of time back in the resort, but having to return to London within the next couple of weeks suited him. It would be a good opportunity to make himself scarce, after what he'd got planned.

Rex was on edge as soon as Edward walked through the door, like a man who thought he'd forgotten a wedding booking. The fear on his face was almost laughable.

'Good morning Rex. You look like you've had a fright.'

'No, er... good morning Mr Callow, it's lovely to see you here. You don't have a meeting scheduled here today, do you? I don't have anything in the booking diary.'

'No, this is an informal visit,' Edward replied, enjoying Rex's discomfort. He had plans for this man too.

'Can I get you anything? Please take a seat in the lounge. I'll get Isla to fetch you a filter coffee.'

'That will be great, thank you.'

Edward moved into the lounge where the last of the late-breakfasting guests were still chatting and reading the papers. Edward found a table that was set but unused and angled himself so he could look out across the bay through the large front window. Morecambe was busy, with the tourists out in force already. Soon the schools would be back, and things would begin to get quieter. Edward preferred the resort when the tourists weren't there.

He looked at his watch; Bob Moseley was due any moment. Punctual almost to the second, he walked into the lounge.

Bob was a man of relatively few words. Edward thought it must be painful for him to speak. He shook Bob's hand and invited him to take a seat.

'Tell me, Bob, how did you and Harvey Turnbull become acquainted?'

Edward liked getting straight to the point. He wasn't one for pleasantries, though they were necessary for his parliamentary work.

'Like everybody he works with, he has dirt on me. That man could see me in jail with the nod of his head. If he wasn't a crooked cop, I'd be rotting in a cell right now. He offered me a deal, and I took it. He also showed me how not to get caught by his colleagues. He pays reasonably well, and he doesn't call on my services very often. It suits me.'

'What happened to your neck?'

'A stupid fight in a bar. Some weedy shit sliced my throat with a broken bottle; it almost killed me. Now I get to speak like Bonnie Tyler on testosterone. Local legend has it I was stabbed with a knife. It sounds better, and I don't challenge it. But I got caught off guard when I wasn't expecting it. That was the first and last time I got caught unawares like that.'

'How would you like to come and work for me?'

Edward spotted it: even a hardened criminal like Bob Moseley had a telling sign. His was a deep swallow.

'What do you mean?'

'Well, I pay Harvey and Harvey pays you. What would you say if I suggested cutting out the middle man?'

'What would happen to Turnbull?' Bob asked.

Edward studied his face. He wanted to know how loyal Bob was to Harvey Turnbull.

'What do you think should happen to Harvey Turnbull?' Edward replied.

'Turnbull holds a gun to my head every day. I do the work, he pays me, I stay out of jail. He's the one person who can ruin my life; he knows everything about me. It would be a considerable relief if that stress was gone. I have a wife and daughter to think about.'

Edward held back a smile. It never ceased to amuse him how men as violent as Bob Moseley could be doting fathers and husbands too. The fact that he'd only recently abducted and imprisoned Jenna Phillips' daughter seemed to be lost on Bob. Perhaps the man had no sense of irony.

'What if I were to offer you a pay rise?' Edward suggested. 'Say, three times what Harvey pays you? Always in cash, and I'll keep you on retainer. I anticipate a busy period for you in the next couple of weeks. Then things will go quiet. I'm reorganising the business, making a few personnel changes.'

Edward's coffee had arrived, served by Rex's assistant. Isla, if he recalled correctly. She moved around the place like a breeze, everywhere at once, nowhere out of bounds. She seemed to have a hand in everything at Lakes View.

Bob nodded. He'd got Edward's meaning. He was considering his own chess board, thinking through his next move.

'Who's that woman?' Edward asked.

'That's Isla Thomas. Her husband and son work out at

sea, in a small fishing boat. She doesn't live far from here. As far as I'm aware, she's worked here for years.'

'Do I need to worry about her?' Edward asked, watching her every move.

'I've never even thought about it. I don't think so. Not so long as she doesn't ask any questions. I think she's pleased to have a job here.'

'So, what do you say?' Edward returned to his subject.

'I think a change of employer could be good. A pay rise would be nice too. Young Maisie is three years old next month. It'll help us to move to a bigger house. And it would be a considerable relief to know that my secrets were buried. Just like this Craven fellow. Some things are best taken care of, in case they cause trouble at a later date.'

Edward smiled at Bob. The man's voice seemed to struggle and fade after excessive use. He wondered what it must be like to deal with an issue like that on a daily basis. But Bob had made his own aggressive chess move, and in a single swipe, he'd removed Harvey Turnbull from the board.

'I'll tell you when,' Edward said. 'I'll leave you to think of something dramatic. The sort of thing that might befall a police officer who's under too much stress. The type of police officer who might have been involved with the abduction of a local schoolgirl. That must be a traumatic experience.'

Bob Moseley nodded and stood up.

'I'm sure I can think of a fitting way to hand in my notice,' he said with a smile.

As Edward took a sip of his coffee and watched Bob walk down the path outside, he caught sight of Isla Thomas passing by in the corridor. Something about her movement made him stop. He gave it a couple of minutes while he finished his drink, then stood up, pushed his chair in and walked out into the corridor. There was no sign of Isla.

The same uneasy feeling compelled him to walk up the stairs to the first floor, then beyond that right to the upper level of the building. It was quiet, too quiet. Isla's movement had bothered him too, the way she'd given him a quick glance as if checking his whereabouts.

Edward had reached the room where Piper Phillips was being held. He listened but could hear nothing. Still, his gut told him to wait a little longer. He stepped back across the landing, lurking in a shadowy area poorly lit by the single ceiling light.

His patience was soon rewarded. The door handle moved quietly, and the door began to open.

Edward was not a violent man, nor was he quick to anger. He always preferred to think things through before acting. But when he saw Isla Thomas walking out of that room, he knew without a shadow of a doubt he needed to take strong, instant action.

Edward pounced, the fingers of his right hand poised to push against her throat. The moment he made contact, without uttering a sound, he launched Isla back into the room, pushed her to the floor and forced his hand down in a deadly grip on her throat.

He knew his face was burning, but the sensation of power it gave him was exhilarating.

'Now tell me what you've seen and heard, you bitch. And don't even think about lying to me.'

CHAPTER THIRTY-ONE

Morecambe - Present Day

Charlotte rushed to the rear end of the containers and threw up, her eyes throbbing in her efforts to stay quiet. This made her sick to her core. Edward Callow was involved in people smuggling. Why the hell did a man with his power and influence need to get involved with something like this?

She'd read about this in the papers: refugees being smuggled in or out of the country in refrigerated containers, a trick to prevent the sniffer dogs from identifying the offending lorries. The vehicle would be packed with terrified people, each one risking their life in a desperate attempt to escape from whichever country they'd come from. Or was it even worse: modern-day slavery?

Charlotte's body convulsed, but her stomach was too empty to vomit again. This was worse than anything she imagined. Edward Callow was a local MP, a property developer and investor; what was he doing lurking in the shadows at Heysham Port?

She had to get a grip on her emotions; becoming hysterical wouldn't help Lucia. She wiped her mouth with her sleeve and took deep breaths. She was familiar with the rush of overwhelming anxiety, a whirlwind of panic. But these men weren't going to take her sanity from her. She'd almost had it stolen from her once before, and she couldn't let it happen again.

Charlotte moved to the front of the container again, taking care to note the positions of the men. Edward had vanished, and the driver appeared to be sealing the door. Charlotte knew from TV and newspapers that lorries were monitored and checked; she assumed what he was doing was connected with this process. But was the lorry going through the docks or had it passed through already? And was Lucia in that truck? Would a man as ruthless as Edward Callow do something as terrible as that?

After killing his own business partners, her daughter would mean absolutely nothing to him. She felt in her pocket for the hammer. If the chance came, she'd willingly kill the man with her own hands.

Her options were limited. If only she hadn't told Nigel Davies to hold off contacting the police for so long. Would he ignore her? She hoped so, but she doubted it. Nigel knew her well enough already to take her at her word.

What should she do next? Her phone was shot, there was no way she could raise the alarm without giving away her presence, and the police weren't due to arrive yet. She'd painted herself into a corner.

Since getting out of the car, she hadn't taken time to examine her surroundings. If she could find a way to the port and alert security or an official, she could bring an end to this.

The lorry was revving now, meaning they were getting ready to move. Charlotte returned to the rear of the containers and took a closer look to see if she could do anything to raise the alarm.

The containers were stacked five rows wide, piled up within a high fence running around the entire perimeter of the storage area. The barrier was solid, constructed of sturdy metal bars, with angle spikes at the top. For a few moments, she considered the possibility of climbing up onto the top of one of the containers and trying to leap from there over the fence. That would be crazy; if she didn't jump far enough, they'd find her impaled on the fence. She wasn't so frantic as to give it more than two seconds of thought.

Her only option was to try for the gates at the front of the compound. She knew before she even looked that her chances of making it out that way were remote, but she had to give it a try.

Working her way along the fencing, concealed at the rear of the first row of containers, Charlotte moved towards the well-lit area at the front of the compound. The lorry was outside the double gates now. All four men were there, and they seemed to be having a word with the driver. Charlotte cursed at not being able to make a note of the number plate or details of the vehicle. What if they'd already passed through the port and were heading out towards the motorway? Those poor people could be dead by the time the police located the lorry. Lucia could be dead.

Everything in her mind was screaming at her to take whatever chance she needed to take. But her rational voice told her to remain steady, to figure it out and find a way to get to her daughter.

Rex was the key. She wasn't alone; there were two of them. And the cars were still there. Had they taken the keys? She didn't know, but why would they, in a secure area? She could rescue Rex, steal a car, drive through the gates and raise the alarm. She had her plan.

Rushing now, eager to bite the bullet, Charlotte retraced her steps along the fence back to the container where she'd left her phone, glad she could recall its where-abouts. If she got out of here, she'd need to tell the police where it was. She was ready to tell DCI Summers every-thing now, whatever the outcome, even if there was a risk of ending up in jail. It had to end. She would never forgive herself for putting her children through all this.

She moved towards the cars, checking that the coast was clear. There was still some activity by the main gates, so this was the perfect time to rescue Rex. But all the containers looked the same. Which one was he in? She walked up and down, then spotted where it might be. There were two blue units next to each other, but she couldn't recall which one he was locked in.

Charlotte tried the first, but it was padlocked, so she moved to the next one, making sure the coast was still clear. It was too difficult to make out what was going on at the gate from that distance. She worked at the mechanism to try to get the door open. Even though she'd done it once before, she still struggled.

At last, she moved the bars in the right direction, and the door began to open. The moment she pulled it outward, Rex stormed at her from inside, knocking her on to the ground outside.

'Jesus, Rex, stop, it's me!'

He thrashed about wildly, ready to punch her in the face, then suddenly stopped as he recognised her. A band of silver tape was still round his neck, but he'd succeeded in tearing away the plastic bag.

'I'm sorry, Charlotte, I'm so sorry. I thought you were them coming back for me. I told them where the video is hidden. I'm so sorry.'

'Rex, it doesn't matter. We have to move fast. The police are coming, but they won't be here for a while longer. We have to do something, now. There's a lorry; there are people trapped in there. They're people-smuggling, I believe. I think Lucia might be in there.'

'They're taking a shipment out of the country. I heard them while they were in the back of the car. They're coming for you and your family, Charlotte. They kept talking about you knowing too much. It all comes back to this Craven man; they're trying to erase history, I think.'

'I have to trust that Will and Olli are safe. DCI Summers promised she'd protect them. Besides, I don't think there are any more of them; everybody is there, by the entrance. If we can raise the alarm, the police will catch them at it.'

'What's your plan?' Rex asked. He winced as he got up from the ground.

'How badly hurt are you?' Charlotte asked. She'd forgotten he'd received a beating; the poor light concealed the bruising to his face.

'Those bastards know what they're doing. That guy with the sore throat can land a punch. I'm sore; it hurts bad, but I can walk, and I can help. What do you want me to do?'

'One moment,' Charlotte said. It was only a matter of hours ago that she'd been pulled from the sea. Now, here she was, planning an audacious escape from the compound.

She hadn't stopped long enough to think about her own wounds. When she did, she realised she was raw, stiff and in some pain. But she didn't care; where Lucia's safety was concerned, it didn't matter.

Looking ahead at the gate, she moved to the first car, checking to see if the keys had been left in; they had. She checked the second vehicle while Rex dusted himself down, getting ready for whatever was coming. The keys were in the ignition once again.

'I don't know how many years it is since you last drove, but we're busting out of this compound. So long as you can steer it in a straight line, it doesn't matter too much what you do with the car—'

Rex wasn't looking at her. He was looking beyond her. She turned.

'And that's far enough,' came a man's voice. She could see the silhouette of his Mohican haircut even before she saw his face. It was the man who'd taken her daughter and tried to kill her husband. And now he was pointing a gun at them.

CHAPTER THIRTY-TWO

Morecambe - Present Day

'You little bastard!' Charlotte seethed, turning to run at the man.

'Callow already wants you dead,' the smirking man replied. 'I suggest you don't give me an excuse to pull this trigger.'

'Charlotte,' Rex warned.

'Why the fuck aren't you dead, old man? We taped that bag tight enough.'

He stepped out of the shadow cast by the container, smirking at them. Charlotte wanted to smash his face in. She moved her hand to her back pocket; the hammer was still there.

Rex gave her a slight nod. He'd seen the hammer.

'Who the hell are you?' she yelled. 'What did you do with my daughter?'

'I'll tell you something, you're a bloody fast runner for an old bird. You should enter the oldies Olympics, the way you chased me on Saturday morning. I was fair out of breath.'

'I'd have wrung your neck if I'd have caught you, you—' Charlotte began.

'Steady,' Rex warned. His eyes were on the handgun.

'How do you know Lucia?' Charlotte asked, heeding Rex's advice.

'She's a sweet little thing. Quite the young woman you've got there. A lovely, friendly young lady. Very trusting too.'

Charlotte felt a rage beginning to rise. She held his gaze, searching his eyes, hating him and wanting to destroy him.

'Is she safe?'

'Depends what you mean by safe,' he replied. 'If you mean, is she dead or in immediate danger, then the answer is no. But if you mean is she safe in the more general sense, I guess the answer would have to be no. Shame though, she's a sweet little kisser, that girl of yours.'

Charlotte had never known hate like it, burning through her as if her blood had turned to molten lava, wanting to tear this man to pieces with her fingers.

'How's that hand of yours?' Charlotte asked. She needed to steer this conversation, or she was in danger of losing her mind.

'Not bad for an old boy. I look forward to getting my revenge on him. And I will. I'm a vicious little git; even my primary school teacher used to say so. Whatever he does to me, I'll give him pain ten times worse. And I won't be quick about it either. I'll let him linger for a while before I put him out of his misery. It's more fun that way. Does he know I fucked your daughter? She wanted it too. Almost begged me for it.'

It was all Charlotte could do not to scream at him. She

had to trust Lucia had more sense, that she hadn't been fooled by this horrible man. She'd had every advantage with Will as her father; surely she could tell the difference between a good man and an evil man. Maybe this monster was Lucia's Bruce Craven.

'What's your name?' Charlotte asked. 'At least tell me who I can curse when I send you to hell.'

'Whatever, potty mouth,' he replied. 'Just call me Tyler. That's what your daughter shouted when we were doing it in one of your guest rooms. The beds are rather lumpy, by the way. You need to think about fixing that.'

'So what's the plan, Tyler?' Rex asked, breaking his silence. Charlotte let him take the lead.

'Well, fat man, for one I'm going to make sure you're finished off properly. But without this feisty lady to come to the rescue, I expect you'll do the decent thing and die this time. By the way, I had a great idea. We're dumping your body in that shop when we burn it. They'll think it was a prison fugitive hiding there. It seems a fitting place to get rid of your stinking, fat body. Edward liked that idea. I got myself a few brownie points, I did.'

'And what about her?' Rex asked. 'What happens to Charlotte? She's done nothing to hurt you.'

Tyler laughed.

'Since when did that matter? Edward Callow is retiring. All loose ends are getting tidied up. He's cleaning up his mess. That Jenna bitch says you knew Bruce Craven. That means you have to go. Simple as that.'

'What do you think will happen to you?' Charlotte asked. She'd taken two steps forward while Rex had been distracting him. She suspected there wasn't a lot going on in the intellect department for Tyler. He was easily diverted.

'What do you mean? I'm a star pupil tonight. Nothing will happen to me.'

'Well, if Edward is tidying up his loose ends, aren't you one of them?'

Charlotte could see that comment had hit the mark. Tyler hadn't thought too far ahead about his career prospects.

'I'll be all right. Besides, I've got plans for you before you get the bullet. I've always fancied a bit of MILF. Let's see if it's like daughter, like mother—'

Tyler lunged towards Charlotte, but her hand was already on the hammer in her pocket. She drew it, flipped it in her hand and smacked Tyler at the side of his head. She felt the thud of metal on a skull, a dead, solid sound. Tyler was still for a moment, then the gun dropped from his left hand. He looked like he was about to shout and raise the alarm, but his legs crumpled, and he fell to the ground.

'Oh shit, is he dead? Have I killed him?'

Rex ran up to Tyler's body, kneeling at his side. He put his hand on Tyler's wrist, searching for a pulse. As he did so, Tyler turned and grasped the back of Rex's neck with his left hand, steadying himself with his right hand. It took Rex by surprise, but Charlotte reacted quickly. She jumped up into the air and landed on Tyler's bandaged hand. He let out a yowl of pain, but Charlotte stamped on it once again.

Rex had recovered now, putting his hand on the crest of Tyler's Mohican and grasping the mound of hair. He jerked Tyler's head from side to side, cursing him.

Charlotte seized the opportunity and picked up the gun.

'We have to move fast, Rex; they'll be coming for us. Put Tyler in that container; he'll be safe enough in there.'

Charlotte pointed the gun at him, and Rex dragged him

by his hair, throwing him into the container. He moved the handles expertly, locking Tyler inside.

'What now?' Rex asked.

'Same plan,' Charlotte replied. 'Wait, he's dropped his phone.'

She ran across to where she'd struck Tyler. A simple phone had been dropped into the oily mud.

'This is a bit old for a young kid like him,' she said, holding it in her free hand.

'You're not intending to use that thing, are you?' Rex asked.

'What, the phone or the gun? I intend to use one of them, and I hope I don't have to use the other.'

'That phone is a burner,' Rex told her. 'Lots of the guys had them in prison. You buy them, then throw them away. That's why it looks so bad.'

'There's movement at the gate,' Charlotte observed. 'I think they're locking us in. They'll be coming to round us up; they must have heard Tyler screaming. Are you ready?'

'As ready as I'll ever be. Good luck Charlotte. If I get out of this in one piece, I'd like to share a toast with you in the guest house. Good luck with finding your daughter.'

Rex moved towards the closest car and got into the driver's seat. Charlotte could see him checking out the controls. She looked ahead; there were two silhouettes making their way towards them slowly, swaggering along the gap between the containers. Rex had started up his vehicle and was attempting to turn it. Charlotte got into the second vehicle, placed the gun on the passenger seat and started up the engine. She had to place a call; this was for DCI Summers to resolve now. She didn't know any phone numbers; she usually relied on autodial. 999 it was.

'Police,' she answered when the prompt came, gripping

the phone between her chin and shoulder as she tried to drive. 'Ambulance. Send an ambulance. Heysham Port. You're looking for a lorry with a container on the back. It's one of those refrigerated ones. And bring marksmen. They have guns.'

Charlotte didn't wait to finish the call. The operator had all the information he needed. With the distance between Morecambe police station and Heysham Port, she reckoned on a ten minute response time if they floored it and came fast. She hadn't a clue what happened when the police sent their shooters out. She'd soon find out, no doubt.

Rex and she were now levelled up, facing the closed gateway ahead in front of them, the figures of two men carrying guns in silhouette straight ahead. She looked across to Rex, who was waiting for her cue. Charlotte revved the engine, then gave a wave to Rex. Ten minutes. That's the time she had to stay alive. She had ten minutes to get to her daughter before the police arrived.

CHAPTER THIRTY-THREE

Morecambe - 2006

'Jesus Christ, Harvey, you've gone too far this time.'

Edward couldn't contain his anger. The front-page headline of The Bay View Weekly was staring out at him, as if pointing an accusing finger:

Morecambe Bay Tragedy: Popular Father And Son Fishing Duo Lost At Sea.

'I told you I had it handled, you prick. What did you have to go and do a stupid thing like this for?'

Harvey Turnbull looked sheepish for a change. He might well be ashamed. He'd made a terrible error of judgement.

Edward and Harvey were walking along the far end of the promenade, towards Hest Bank. They'd both parked at Happy Mount Park car park, after Edward had issued an immediate summons. Harvey's rash actions could screw up everything.

'When you told me she'd been in to see the girl, I thought we had to send a strong shot across her boughs—'

'You drowned her husband and son at sea, you fucking idiot!'

Edward could barely contain his rage enough to get his words out. If only he had the physical superiority to beat Harvey Turnbull to a pulp.

'To be fair, that wasn't what I asked for when I ordered it to—'

'I don't give a shit what you asked for. Isla Thomas has nothing left now. She's lost everything, thanks to you and that blundering idiot you sent out to sea to give them a fright.'

'It was an accident, Edward.'

'It could bring everything tumbling down. Everything we've built, everything I've worked for. How the hell did your man end up drowning them? How incompetent do you need to be to mess up a job as badly as that?'

'It went very wrong, I admit it. But the boat was lost at sea. It was too far out in deep waters for them to warrant sending out teams to retrieve the bodies. It was meant to be a small, onboard fire, a warning. How could my man know the engine was leaking fuel? He said it went up in a ball of flames. He suffered minor burns himself.'

'I don't care what happened to your man. In fact, he needs to disappear; soon, I'd suggest. The entire bloody town is mourning these guys: the fishing community, local councillors, everybody. I'll have to go to the memorial service myself; as the local MP, I can't be absent. And all the time I'm standing there with my solemn face, I'll be thinking of the imbecile who caused those deaths.'

'I promise, Edward, this will not come back to us. It's been written off as a tragic engine fire at sea, an accident.

The coroner will confirm that. I know how these things play out. Isla Thomas was a dangerous woman.'

Noticing a dog walker approaching, Harvey had lowered his voice.

'Good morning.' Edward greeted her with a cheery tone.

'Oh, hello, Mr Callow. You're doing an excellent job as our local MP. I'll be sure to vote for you again next time!'

'That's very kind of you,' Edward replied.

The two men walked on. As soon as they were out of earshot, Edward continued his conversation with Harvey.

'I told you I'd dealt with Isla Thomas. I'd scared her off, given her a warning. She wasn't going to cause any trouble.'

'But she knew we had the girl in there. What if she reported it to the police?'

'We've already agreed Rex Emery is the fall guy. There's no way of tracing it back to us; the girl hasn't seen any of us. We can release her in the town, and it'll all be over. We've put the frighteners on Jenna Phillips; she assures me Bruce Craven has gone. She did mention another couple that knew him, but they're long gone; they moved away from the area. You messed this up badly, Harvey. You'd better fix it.'

Edward would never have admitted it to Harvey, but he too had been at a loss about what to do about Isla Thomas. She was a loose cannon. She'd assured Edward she was only in the room to check the sheets were fresh and that it had been aired. He had his hands round her throat at the time, her face was bright red, and she was struggling to breathe. He was as certain as he could be that she was telling the truth, but he didn't like the woman. She seemed to be every-where in that guest house.

He'd discovered something new about himself in the

encounter with Isla: it felt good to frighten someone. He could see now how people like Harvey Turnbull got a taste for it. Edward had spent much of his younger life at the mercy of bullies. Then he'd turned their psychotic tendencies to his advantage, getting the crazy, violent men to work for him.

But he'd known a new sensation when he was squeezing Isla Thomas's neck, watching the sheer terror in her eyes, feeling the life draining from her body. She'd thought he was going to kill her. For a period of about three seconds, he was; he wondered what it would be like.

In the end, he'd released his hand and let her have her life back. He'd sent her on her way with a warning, making her swear she'd stay away from the room, which he claimed was being used for a private business matter. But the sense of power over life and death in their encounter had made him feel godlike, and he wanted to experience that elation and adrenaline flow once again.

As Harvey walked alongside, spouting more bullshit about how the deaths couldn't be linked to them, Edward came up with a plan of his own. It was time to tidy up some loose ends: Isla Thomas, Jenna Phillips, Harvey Turnbull,... and the idiot who Harvey had paid to fire a flare directly at the fishing boat as a threat.

'How do you plan to get rid of the fool who destroyed their boat?' Edward asked. He wanted Harvey to sort out his own mess before he took matters into his own hands. Bob Moseley was on Edward's payroll now, and he was awaiting his first instructions.

'Suicide,' Harvey answered. At least he'd already worked out his response. 'As I told you, I got him to call in the fire as a cover. He's the hero of the hour. It was neater if he claimed to have seen the fire, gone to help them, failed and returned to report the incident. It accounts for his presence out there. He has to fish those waters too.'

They stopped walking, and Edward looked out across the bay, scanning for any sign of boats. It was something he'd never paid attention to, even though he knew there was still a community of fishermen based in Morecambe.

'He'll be found hanged in his boat,' Harvey continued. 'The official reason will be that he was distressed at not being to help two of his fellow fishermen. We'll even leave a little note, saying as much. I'm telling you, Edward, this will all go away. The fishing community are used to losing their own. The local paper will love the double tragedy angle. There'll be a big fuss; then it will all blow over.'

'I want it dealt with quickly. I also want you to find the girl and make Rex Emery the fall guy. We're in danger of this slipping away from us. We can't let that happen.'

'What then?' Harvey asked. 'Where do we go from there?'

'You said the Newcastle cops have drawn a blank with Bruce Craven?'

'They're closing the case. It's been a dead-end for them. There's no paperwork they can access to trace staff at the holiday camp. The company went bust in the end. Bob Moseley has scared Jenna Phillips witless; she thought she'd never see him and Neil Carthy again after they paid her that first visit when she was a teenager. Bob said he'd loved us to have seen her face. She was so scared, she wet herself. She knows we have her daughter, she's terrified, and she wants us out of her life. She realises that if she breathes a word of it to my colleagues at the police station, she'll never see her daughter again. We can close the door on this one if we make Rex Emery the fall guy, though we'll have to find a new meeting place. I've got a feeling that dump of a guest house will be closing soon.'

'Well, there are plenty of other hotels; they're two-a-penny in Morecambe,' Edward replied, now satisfied Harvey had things under control.

'What about Isla Thomas?' Harvey asked. 'Is she still a danger? Do I need to sort her out?'

Edward was looking out across the bay. It was a beautiful place, so peaceful and scenic. He was pleased he'd decided to make his life in the resort.

'She just lost her son and husband. I'd say that's punishment enough, wouldn't you? We'll let her get the two of them buried. She can have her memorial service with the whole town crying their eyes out. Then she can have another warning. She's seen what the stakes are, and she realises she's playing with fire if she tries to come for us. I think she's had enough for now, don't you?'

Edward believed himself to be a merciful God. He truly believed Isla would keep her mouth shut after the trauma that had wrecked her life. And to make certain, she and Jenna Phillips would be treated to a little spectacle; the death of Harvey Turnbull.

CHAPTER THIRTY-FOUR

Morecambe - Present Day

Charlotte gave a signal to Rex Emery then released the handbrake. To her right, after an uncertain start, Rex got his car moving. They sped along the gap between the containers, roughly side by side, heading straight for the two men who were walking towards them. The only plan she had was to smash through the gates and get out of that compound.

She hadn't expected the two men to go on the offensive so fast. In Charlotte's head, it would play out like a movie. They'd roar towards the gate, a perfect distance between the cars, and the two men would leap out of the way. Then they'd crash through the gates, which would obligingly be knocked off their hinges, and she'd intercept the lorry and save her daughter. That tableau was playing through her mind even as she saw the men standing confidently in front of them, guns drawn and ready to fire at their windscreens.

Charlotte floored the accelerator, then thought better of

it. She hated it when she ran over a rabbit or squirrel on a country lane, so there was no way she could crash through those men. By their confident stance, it looked like they had a pretty good understanding of that too.

She glanced across at Rex, but before she had a chance to catch his eye, the shooting began. They were calm and confident, as if they'd shot at moving targets a thousand times before. She couldn't even hear the shots, but she saw the first impact on Rex's windscreen as a bullet struck the glass.

Rex veered towards her, as if his change in direction would stop the bullet meant for her, and struck the rear of Charlotte's vehicle. Reacting to the collision, Charlotte swerved to the left, clipping a container and then fighting to gain full control of the car. As she straightened up, she glanced in her rear-view mirror to see if Rex had been hurt. He was still driving, albeit more slowly.

The two men ahead were standing firm. Charlotte was less than one hundred yards away from them now. She gritted her teeth as she neared them, watching as they levelled their guns at her.

Two shots rang out, and the car sank beneath her as the two front tyres deflated. Amid the loose flapping of shredded rubber, the car started to weave from one side to the other. She clipped another container, and the car stopped dead, catapulting her forward.

A white cloud appeared in front of her, in slow motion, and her face met it. The airbag had stopped her forward movement, but the momentum lifted her body off the seat then sent it crashing back down again.

Charlotte was dazed and shaken. An excruciating pain burned in her left shoulder, making her scream in agony at the slightest movement. A bone was sticking out below her shoulder blade; she must have dislocated her shoulder.

The gun. The one she'd taken from Tyler. Where was it? She lurched towards the passenger side footwell, trying to find it, howling in pain, scared that she might pass out. Lucia. She had to get to Lucia. The man with the gravelly voice was speaking. Where was Rex? Had they shot him?

Charlotte's hand found the solid metal of the gun's grip and picked it up, staying low in the footwell. She hadn't a clue what to do with it.

'Steady,' the man with the raw voice said.

All she could do was work out how to fire the gun, then run for her life. What a botched mess of an escape plan. But where was Rex?

The second man cursed.

'Where the fuck did he come from—?'

There was a crunch on the driver's side of her car, sending the vehicle spinning to the side. Charlotte cried out as her left shoulder slammed against the fascia, and her head struck the side of the steering wheel. At the same time, there was a deep thud on the car roof. Then a bloody face crashed on to the car windscreen from above. Rex had slammed his car into one of the men, it had sent him flying into the air.

As the dead eyes of a corpse stared at her through the glass, the air vanished from her lungs and fear paralysed her. She could only stare in horror at the bloodied body.

A drip of blood trickled out of the man's mouth on to the windscreen. That minute detail helped her to snap her mind back to the most pressing issue: survival.

The smash had forced the passenger side door open. If she could take the pain it would cause, she would be able to get out that way. A car was revving; it had to be Rex. He must be coming back to help her.

Charlotte clung on to the gun, and lunged forward, letting out an agonised cry as the pain gripped her again. How much longer could she carry on?.

She pulled herself out of the car using only her right arm, still hanging on to the gun, then dropped to the ground. As she pulled herself up, her eyes streamed with tears at the sheer agony of it.

The second man's body was strewn across the bonnet of the car she'd been driving. His left leg was snapped back; there was no way he could still be alive. The other man was nowhere to be seen. And several hundred yards away, the engine still revving, was the car that Rex Emery was driving. He was crunching the gears, turning it, hopefully coming back to pick her up. But where was the man with the gravelly voice? He had a gun.

Charlotte looked around, desperate to find him in the semi-darkness. He could be anywhere.

Then she spotted the second man's gun on the ground. It would be ready to fire. She dropped her own weapon and moved into the strip between the containers, still in pain. She picked up the firearm and scanned the gaps between the containers. It was useless; the other man could be anywhere.

The car had come to rest near one of the storage units. She could climb from the car roof to the top of the container, from where she'd be able to see the last of Callow's bully boys.

Grimacing at the pain and trying to blot out the sight of the dead body, Charlotte pulled herself up on the boot and then onto the roof of the car. She steadied herself. Then, bracing herself against the pain, she jumped towards the top of the container. There was another gunshot in the distance. She landed badly, crying at the searing pain shooting through her left shoulder.

Something was different now. It was quieter. The car Rex had been driving was no longer being revved.

CHAPTER THIRTY-FIVE

Morecambe - Present Day

The top of the container provided a view across several rows in the compound, apart from where they were piled two or three high. Charlotte scanned the immediate area and heard the engine turning over, several containers away. Rex was alive at least, but it sounded like he was having trouble getting the car started.

Then, just ahead, Charlotte saw a moving shadow. Immediately alert, she placed her finger on the trigger of the weapon. How long would it be until the police arrived? She wasn't sure how much more of this she could take.

Seeing the shadow disappear, she moved to the edge of the container roof, wary, glancing around. There was no movement anywhere.

Charlotte registered the flash before she heard the sound. A single bullet struck the metal unit below her feet, making her stumble backwards. She fell hard, jarring her shoulder as she reached out to break her fall, rolling around crying from the pain, unable to stop the tears streaming down her face.

She'd seen how shoulders were pushed back into place on television; was it worth a try? They made it look so easy. But the muscles surrounding her shoulder felt torn. It would probably still hurt as much if it was back in place. The thought of it made her legs go weak.

Charlotte rolled on to her right-hand side, letting go of the gun so she could get back on her feet and keeping low in case the man who'd fired was scouring the area for her. She daren't return to ground level. Shuffling towards the edge of the container, she tried to work out whether the distance to the next one was narrow enough to leap across.

A shadow passed across two units directly ahead of her. Once on the ground, he would be the hunter and she would be the prey. Even if she could pull the trigger on the gun, she had little hope of hitting her target. And even though they had her daughter, Charlotte was no killer. If they forced her, if they gave her no other choice, she would take a life. But she still couldn't imagine doing it.

Far in the distance, Charlotte thought she heard a helicopter; was she imagining it? Were the police here at last? She should have told Nigel Davies to alert them earlier. She was no match for these men. They were killers.

Charlotte looked out across the containers again. She had a clear run of five, which would almost take her as far as Rex Emery's car. If she could make it across that distance, at least she'd be able to get a decent view of her opponent.

She backed up and checked where the far edge was, so she didn't mess up the jump. This would hurt like hell, but it was better than a bullet to the head. She took a deep breath, then paused. The gun was best out of her hand as she landed.

Tucking the gun into the waistband of her jeans, she prepared herself for the run. She knew nothing about safety catches, but she figured the weapon was safe so long as she kept clear of the trigger. Then she caught sight of her pursuer below; he was getting ready to fire. A gunshot rang out as she launched herself across the roof of the container and into the air. Even as she leapt, she felt her left arm convulse, but she had no other choice. She was running for her life.

Charlotte landed on the roof of the opposite container, crashing down and trying to ignore the excruciating pain as she prepared to jump again.

The man with the gun was following her progress, training his weapon on her. She landed on the next container, this time letting out a scream of both frustration and agony, but she had to keep moving. Could she outrun him?

There were two more containers to go; she'd have to stop soon. The units were piled three high after that. There was another shot. It was a race to kill her before the police got there. Who even knew where that scumbag Edward Callow was?

She jumped again, almost landing short this time, feeling herself flagging. There was only one container remaining. The man was still behind her, but he had the advantage of being able to shoot. She'd have to jump off the container at the end of the row; why hadn't she thought of that? It was high, too high with her current injuries. The chances of her landing on the ground without breaking her ankle, or at the very least spraining it, were minimal.

Charlotte ran anyway and made the jump, landing badly and rolling across the top of the last container, the momentum spinning her as she fell and her legs failed to support her. Landing on her right side, she almost rolled off the edge but managed to stop the spin in time. At the sound of another gunshot, she stayed low, every joint in her body screaming at her to stop.

There was a roar up ahead; Rex had got the car going. Thank goodness the man with the hideous voice had chosen to target her instead of Rex; at least she'd provided a distraction whilst Rex had got the car started again. In the distance, the helicopter was growing louder, as if it was swooping across the port area, hopefully searching for them.

As silently as she could, Charlotte moved to the end of the container closest to Rex, keeping her head low. She could hear the man who was hunting her, but he was too close to see her. He would have his gun ready; the moment he spotted her, he would shoot.

She waved her right hand at Rex, trying to draw his attention. He was revving the car, no doubt working out his own plan of action. He flashed the headlights; he'd seen her. She put up her hand to signal, then beckoned him over. If she could leap off the roof of the unit onto the car, it would be easier to get to the ground. Then they could break out of the compound and put themselves into the safe hands of the police.

Rex had understood her cue. He let out the clutch, and the car skidded a little in the mud, then headed straight for her container. He braked suddenly as he came alongside it, and Charlotte stood up to make one final leap onto the roof of the car, yelling again in pain.

She'd been too sure of herself. The car roof seemed easy compared with the leaps she'd made previously, but her right foot only just made it and as she tried to steady herself, she slipped and fell off.

Rex called to her from the car, his voice clear. Either his

window was wound down, or it had been shot out. The helicopter was overhead now, and a flashlight was moving around the containers, searching them out. At last, help had arrived.

There was a crunch to her side, then a single shot, and Rex was silent. The car lurched and stopped. Lying on the ground, trying to control the pain in her left arm, she turned and saw two feet next to her head. She looked up slowly. It was the man with the gravelly voice, his gun pointing directly at her.

'You are one fucking annoying lady,' he said, his voice sounding hoarse and raspy. 'I can't tell you how much pleasure it'll give me, blowing your head to mush.'

CHAPTER THIRTY-SIX

Morecambe - 2006

Edward Callow possessed enough self-awareness to understand that something fundamental changed in his life that day. Some people might claim he'd become a monster. In his view, it was a case of becoming a more effective manager.

Sometimes difficult decisions had to be made when you were at the top. He had a fledgling political career and a lucrative construction company partnership; Harvey Turnbull could not be allowed to jeopardise that at any cost. Nobody would interfere with his plans. He would die fighting to protect what he'd built, rather than go through the ignominy of a public trial and public prosecution. That was why he did what had to be done that day.

Edward placed the newspaper on his kitchen worktop, took a sip of coffee and read the headline one more time.

Third Tragic Bay Death. Fisherman Said To Be 'Haunted' By Deaths At Sea.

At least Turnbull had mopped up his mess. In allowing the original tragedy to happen, he'd made an enemy of Isla Thomas. Sure, she'd be in grief for a while, perhaps even struggling with depression or suicidal feelings after the death of her husband and son at sea. But Turnbull had made her dangerous. And that had to be sorted.

Today would be a busy day, and there was one more job for Harvey Turnbull to do before it was time for him to clear his desk at Morecambe Police Station. Edward picked up his mobile phone and dialled.

'Len, hello, it's Edward Callow.'

He loved his direct line access to the police chief. As prime minister, he'd have it to every police chief, army general, head of industry and world leader. One day. One day he would command that power.

Len Chambers answered expectantly; after all, this was not their first call.

'Hello Mr Callow, good to hear from you. What can I do for you?'

'I wanted to ask if you'd been able to do anything about Harvey Turnbull yet? We met for a social drink earlier this week, and he seemed concerned and distracted. Off the record, he confided in me that he's been experiencing great stress recently and that he's struggling with his workload. I think dealing with the aftermath of those two fishermen was difficult for him. Underneath that tough exterior is a very empathetic man.'

Edward almost burst out laughing at his own words.

'Please don't tell him I told you that, I'm only mentioning it to you as a dear friend of Harvey's and as his local MP.'

'He's been offered support, but he rejected it outright,' Len Chambers replied. 'It's very difficult when a member of staff won't take the help we offer. A lot of older coppers like Harvey take it as a matter of pride. They consider they're failing their colleagues if they take time out or show any weakness. I think that's where we are with Harvey. It's very sad. He's a good officer; in fact, he's about to deliver us a big win today. An arrest for abducting a child. I'm expecting a briefing any time now.'

Edward played dumb, despite knowing exactly what was happening that morning. Rex Emery was about to be stitched up for the abduction and kidnap of Piper Phillips. Harvey Turnbull would be the hero of the hour, responding to an anonymous tip-off. A CD of pornographic images would be found in Rex Emery's guest house. Then it would all go terribly wrong for poor old Harvey Turnbull.

'Well, I felt duty-bound to let you know. Harvey is a good friend of mine. I've known him since I worked at the Town Hall. I have only his best wishes at heart.'

'I appreciate that,' Len Chambers answered. 'It's above and beyond what anybody could expect of their local MP. You'll definitely be getting my vote again whenever we have the next election.'

Edward smiled; sometimes it was too easy. He ended the call to the chief constable and looked at the clock in the kitchen. It ought to be done by now. He switched on the radio and moved the dial to BBC Radio Lancashire. There was a '70s song to tolerate before the news bulletin came on, but as Harvey had promised, the raid would be carried out early, and the media outlets would have the story by ten o'clock.

As the news jingle played, he turned up the volume.

BBC Radio Lancashire news at ten o'clock...

Edward's heart jumped; he was surprised at how excited he felt.

A man has been arrested at the Lakes View Guest House in Morecambe after police acted on an anonymous tip-off that a local girl was being held there against her will. Detective Chief Inspector, Harvey Turnbull, confirmed a sixteen-year-old girl had been found in an attic area within the guest house. The girl, who cannot be named for legal reasons, is now being treated in hospital.

This was good; it was an excellent start to the day. It was almost sad that Harvey had to go. If he hadn't been such an idiot...

Speaking outside the guest house only minutes ago, DCI Turnbull said it was a shocking case.

Edward turned up the radio a little louder to hear Harvey's interview. They'd discussed the wording that Harvey would use. He had no idea what he was setting himself up for.

Cases like this are always disturbing and shocking. They take their toll on officers who are exposed to the most harrowing situations.

Harvey came across well on the radio. He'd be making the headlines again the next day.

In this case, a local girl, aged sixteen, was abducted and held by a man for five days in the Lakes View Guest House.

Edward could hear the press scrum over the radio. A journalist asked Harvey if the owner of the guest house was responsible.

I can confirm a man has been arrested and taken to Morecambe police station for questioning, but he has not yet been charged. I would remind the press this girl is a minor in the eyes of the law and should not be named in your reports. Thank you.

The audio insert into the news bulletin abruptly ended, and the newsreader moved to the next story.

A Morecambe man has cycled the length of the town's promenade on a unicycle...

Edward switched off the radio. So it was done. The girl was free; Emery set up as the fall guy and no mention of the child pornography. That would come out later, at trial. Harvey Turnbull had obtained a CD from another local pervert they'd been investigating and concealed it in the guest house. The job was done.

The rest of that day was spent on constituency matters. As Edward shuffled papers in his office, made calls and arranged meetings, a sense of excitement was building. Ever since he'd threatened violence towards Isla Thomas, he'd felt more alive than ever before. Now he was going to ramp that up and tie up the final loose ends so he could move on.

Just before ten o'clock that night, as Adventure Kingdom was about to shut up for the night, Edward sat on a bench at the far reaches of the leisure park. In the daytime, this was a picnic area, tucked at the back of the park behind the rides. In the dark of the night time, with the entire site lit up by flashing bulbs and the air filled with shouts, screams, mechanical noise and thudding pop music, it gave Edward an excellent view of what was about to happen.

He was dressed as a tourist, an uncomfortable experience he never wanted to repeat, in a baseball cap, jeans, gaudy T-shirt and trainers. The small group assembled ahead of him, unaware he was watching.

Bob Moseley brought in Harvey Turnbull first, hooded and bound. Edward could tell it was Turnbull by his posture. The big dipper flew along the track, in front of Bob. It was the perfect spot to do it. The train made a massive drop, flying round a tight corner where the tracks came near ground level. It passed by so quickly, the people on the ride would still be recovering from the drop and travelling far too fast to see what was coming.

In one confident, forceful move, Bob pushed Harvey on to the track and created a noose around his neck, lashing him to the outer rail. Harvey thrashed about and struggled but was unable to release himself. With a hood over his head like that, Edward wondered how scared he was. Just thinking about it excited him in a way no relationship ever had.

From the gap in the fencing, Neil Carthy arrived, guiding two figures by their arms. They too had light hoods on their heads. Even from that distance, Edward could see Bob was shouting at them. He got the gist of it. He knew what Bob would be saying.

Speak a word, and this will happen to you and those you love. Keep your mouths shut and you'll be fine.

It was the staple fare of intimidation. He didn't have to hear the words to get the sense of it. The big dipper ride had been re-loaded with another set of tourists and was winding its way along the far side of the tracks. Edward reckoned Harvey would be able to feel the vibration along the metal track; it was an exhilarating thought.

Bob and Neil had positioned the two hooded figures a short distance away from Harvey Turnbull. Harvey was still struggling; the piece of shit would be begging for his life. The big dipper train was being dragged up the track, ready to drop at great speed to where Harvey was secured. Edward watched it play out, a smile on his face throughout.

Bob and Neil pulled the hoods off the two witnesses: Isla Thomas and Jenna Phillips. He watched Isla Thomas sink to her knees when she worked out what they were about to witness. The long truck of the big dipper reached the peak and began to gather speed as it began its journey down the other side. Edward didn't dare blink. It would be fast and he didn't want to miss it when it came.

The front truck on the big dipper hit the first turn on the track; the end for Harvey was seconds away. Edward could see Isla Thomas and Jenna Phillips were screaming and shouting, but he could hear nothing above the sounds of the fairground rides.

He saw the wheels as they struck Harvey's neck—he was still struggling right to the end—and he was pleased to see Bob and Neil stepping back into the shadows, on the off-chance anybody on the ride might, by a freak of chance, spot them.

The big dipper truck flew past and was on its way. Harvey Turnbull's decapitated torso had fallen to the ground. Fast and efficiently, Bob removed all signs that Harvey Turnbull had been restrained. The ties binding his hands and ankles were cut away and removed, then thrown inside the hood that had been on his head.

Jenna's hood was replaced. Edward could see her shaking with terror, even at that distance. She looked like a broken woman.

Isla Thomas was still kneeling on the ground, crying and shouting as far as Edward could tell. Bob Moseley replaced the hood on her head, and the two women were escorted away through the gap in the fence.

Edward sat for a few moments and looked at Harvey Turnbull's body, lifeless and still. The man's power had vanished in an instant. Before he stood up and walked away, Edward took a few moments to reflect on the events of that day. All in all, it was a great day's work. All loose ends were sewn up, a thorn in his side had been removed, and it heralded the beginning of a productive future relationship with Bob Moseley. And if Edward had anything to do with it, it would be the first and last day he ever wore a baseball cap.

CHAPTER THIRTY-SEVEN

Morecambe - Present Day

Charlotte tensed, waiting for the moment to come. She hadn't expected it to end like this; in fact, she hadn't considered at all how it might end. She just had to keep on trying, doing anything she could to rescue Lucia.

Her eyes were closed as she listened to the helicopter above them. What else was there to do but wait for the bullet to come? They'd beaten her; those bastards had beaten her. They'd taken her daughter and tried to kill her husband and son. It was over. It was her fault that the police were too late; she'd made the wrong call. She thought she could save Lucia on her own, but she was wrong. She wasn't strong enough.

Charlotte felt something heavy thud against her leg. She opened her eyes and jumped with shock. That monster of a man was lying still on the ground, his gun cast aside. She looked up and spotted the barrel of a rifle protruding from the helicopter above. It was a police marksman; they'd shot him. She raised the hand on her good arm in the air, to show them she wasn't one of them. The helicopter moved away, and she edged back to the car. She could have screamed with delight when she saw Rex Emery moving. He was hurt, wounded in the leg it would seem, but he was conscious.

Charlotte knew nothing about armed police officers, but she'd seen enough crime series on TV to know that if she was spotted with a gun in her hand, they'd likely take her out too. She assumed DCI Summers would have briefed her officers, but she wasn't banking on it. Before she attended to Rex, she made sure that any guns, her own included, were kicked well out of the way. She didn't even want to pick them up. She was done with guns.

'Rex, are you okay?'

She winced as she leaned across the passenger seat.

Rex groaned. 'It hurts like hell... Jesus, Charlotte, your shoulder is dislocated.'

'Tell me about it. I keep thinking I'm going to pass out. How much blood have you lost?'

'It's more the shock of it than anything,' Rex replied. 'Look, we have to get that shoulder sorted. I've done this once before, years ago, in the army. It'll hurt like nothing you've ever experienced before...'

'Couldn't be worse than childbirth.'

'Look, I don't know anything about that, but it'll be painful, okay?'

'I'm going after Lucia,' she said. 'I'm not stopping until the police come and take over.'

'Of course; why do you think I'm offering to put your shoulder back? I'll do your shoulder if you tie my leg. Deal?'

'Deal.'

The helicopter was still buzzing overhead, albeit at a greater distance now. Rex and Charlotte struggled out of the car and moved to the cover of the containers. Rex removed his belt while Charlotte tore off the sleeve from his shirt as best she could with one hand. Then between them, they applied a makeshift dressing and pulled the belt tightly around his open leg wound, Charlotte grimacing throughout as she tugged and twisted.

'Okay, your turn,' Rex said.

It was a pain Charlotte knew had to come, but better sooner than later.

Rex limped behind her and gently placed his hands to the side of her neck, on the dislocated joint. He moved his fingers, as if trying to find the perfect position, then without a word of warning, pushed sharply.

'Oh, Jesus fucking Christ!' Charlotte screamed out. 'You might have warned me. Damn it, that hurt.'

Rex stood back and allowed her to swear and shout. Charlotte couldn't help herself. She ran through every expletive she could think of, tears streaming down her face. However, Rex had done what he said; it was still agonising, but she had control of her arm again.

'Still, childbirth was worse,' she said to Rex once the initial searing pain had passed.

'Then you have my utmost respect and admiration,' he replied. 'I can't imagine what that's like. I'll never complain about man flu ever again.'

Charlotte managed a smile, but her thoughts were on Lucia.

'Promise me you'll rest and stay still,' she urged. 'Don't touch those guns, Rex. You're a fugitive, remember. Move out where they can see you, well away from the guns, and do whatever they say. We'll fix this and prove your innocence. Don't get yourself shot.'

'And you?' he asked.

'They won't shoot me, but I'm not letting that lorry out of here. The moment the cops get here, I'll let them handle it. Are the keys in the car?'

Rex nodded.

'Good luck, Charlotte. I hope you find your daughter.'

She was off, looking up at the helicopter, moving into the driver's seat of the one car that wasn't yet wrecked, though Rex had done a pretty good job of damaging it already. It was liberating to have movement in her left arm back, even if she was still in excruciating pain. It allowed her full movement at least, but there was no way she could lean across to close the passenger side door. It didn't matter; by the time she'd finished, even WeBuyAnyCar wouldn't touch the vehicle.

She fumbled for the car key, which was still in the ignition. It looked like the reason Rex had had trouble starting the car was because he hadn't pressed the start button. The engine roared into life. Charlotte revved it to check it was working, put the engine into gear and drove off, crunching the gears as she moved away.

In her rear-view mirror, she could see the man who'd been shot. As she put the car's lights on full beam, the body of the other man was visible ahead of her, splayed on the shattered, bloody windscreen of the car she'd been driving earlier. She shuddered, relieved she hadn't had to kill anybody, yet now certain she could, if it came to it.

Charlotte had seen cars smashing through locked gates a million times on TV, but as she moved through the gears and picked up speed on her way to the exit, she began to have doubts about whether it would work. But it was her only way out.

The gates looked heavy, with a padlock fastening them together. Those bastards had locked her and Rex in the fenced-off area to round them both up, like caged animals.

Although it seemed she was driving fast, the speed display registered little more than 30 miles per hour. She'd forgotten her seatbelt. Charlotte took her right hand off the wheel, pulled the seatbelt across and clicked it into place.

With seconds to go before impact, the car veered to one side. She raised her left hand to pull it over, cursing with pain. The vehicle straightened up, and she closed her eyes as the bumper struck the metal of the gate. She heard the whoosh of the airbag exploding from the middle of the steering wheel, the crash of metal against metal and a heavy thud on the roof as one of the gates collapsed on it.

Charlotte swore at the airbag that blocked her sight, as the car careered from one side to the next. In a panic, she slammed her foot on the brake. The car screeched to a halt, and she was pushed forward into the airbag as the engine stalled.

Charlotte grabbed a pen from the drinks holder and pierced the airbag. It deflated, like a bedraggled, burst balloon at the end of a kid's party.

Not wasting a second, Charlotte turned the key and started the engine. The flashing lights of police cars appeared at what must be the far end of the docks. The lorry was ahead of her; it looked like it was first in the queue to board the ferry. Lucia was in there, she was certain of it. She turned the car and began to head for the lorry, knowing she was moments away from rescuing her daughter.

As she drove along the road towards the lorry, the mobile phone she'd taken from Tyler earlier began to ring in her back pocket. Twisting awkwardly, she pulled it out with her left hand and answered it. She listened to see who was at the end of the phone.

'Mum? It's Lucia. Stop the car. You need to stop the car now, or he'll kill me.'

CHAPTER THIRTY-EIGHT

Morecambe - Present Day

'Lucia?'

Edward Callow's voice came over the phone speaker.

'Do as she says. You can have your daughter back, but you have to act fast and do exactly as I tell you.'

Charlotte slammed on the brakes, not caring that the car had stalled again, and opened the car door. Behind her, the sirens were wailing. They'd find her soon. The helicopter had been scouring the entire area since the shooting.

'Look up.'

Charlotte obeyed. The car had come to rest at the side of a gigantic container lift, like the huge Transformer toy Olli used to have as a toddler. There were massive rubber wheels on either side of the four supporting pillars. A metal staircase zig-zagged across the sturdy, iron legs, leading to a cage at the top. The docks were lit well enough for her to see that Edward Callow was up there, safely protected by the fencing which ran around a platform mounted at the top.

But Lucia was on the other side of the barrier, hanging on to the railing with both hands. She could just make out Edward's free hand clutching Lucia's top.

'What do you want?' Charlotte asked.

'We need to talk,' Edward replied.

'You let Lucia go, you bastard!'

'I promise you she'll be safe as long as you work with me. I want you to come up those steps and join me here. We're going into the cabin where we can't be seen by that fucking helicopter. One wrong move and I'm throwing her out. I'm not even sure if it's high enough to be certain of a kill; she might spend the remainder of her life in a wheelchair.'

'I'm coming,' Charlotte replied. She didn't want to taunt this man in any way that would put her daughter in danger.

Charlotte left the call open but tucked the phone into her back pocket. She looked up again but could no longer see Lucia. Hoping her daughter was confined safely within the cab at the top, she counted the stairs; there were six flights to navigate. The first flight was movable, like the steps used to board an aeroplane. As she began to climb, she searched for the helicopter; it appeared to be running a circuit of the docks. The police cars were fanning out too. She wished she could remember DCI Summers' phone number.

She ran up the stairs and along a short platform, then started on the second staircase, an integral part of the main structure. The wind was sharper up there, and she hadn't even begun to think about the height. It was one thing using the steps in a block of flats or a high-rise building, but another thing entirely doing it without walls at either side and with the wind getting fiercer the higher she climbed.

The stairs shook and swayed as she made her way up. A man in a hard hat and fluorescent jacket probably made that trip several times a day; for her, it was a daunting challenge.

Thank God there were no ladders; her arm was painful enough.

As she moved from the third staircase to the fourth, two police cars passed on the road beneath and another stopped to investigate her abandoned car. The further she climbed, the more breathless she became, the strength of the wind making it harder to breathe.

What did Edward want? What could he possibly gain now? The game was over, wasn't it?

Charlotte made the mistake of looking down, and her head began to swim. The container lift was heavy and sturdy, but exposed; the higher she got, the scarier it became. She hastily switched to looking upwards, where there was a jumble of moving parts, platforms and cages. There was a clearer view of the platform, on which the control cab must be based. She'd never seen anything like this contraption before, but she'd seen cranes and the massive structures at docks when travelling abroad. They would all be the same.

At the top of the sixth metal staircase, Charlotte reached a small platform, leading to two narrower staircases. These opened out to an outer cage at the top. The moment she stepped in to it, the wind caught her hair. She was now figuring out her route step by step, surrounded by ironwork, gears, chains and machinery. Ahead, on the far platform, was the control cab. As she moved to the relative security of the iron platform, the wind almost blew her off her feet.

Why weren't the police more visible? They seemed to

be focused on the compound where the man had been shot by the marksman. Didn't they know where she was?

She staggered across the platform and up to the cabin. The door was closed, so she decided to knock, ridiculous though it seemed. She didn't want to give Edward Callow any surprises that might spook him.

'Come in!'

She opened the metal door carefully, keen to assess the situation before committing herself. She could see Edward Callow, but not Lucia.

'Where is she, you bastard? I see your little heart problem sorted itself out soon enough.'

Her earlier resolution not to taunt him was broken already.

Edward smiled at her.

'Thanks to my own private doctor. One carefully deployed tranquiliser, and everybody's terrified their local MP has died. I'm pleased with that diversion; it worked very well, even if I say so myself.'

Now she realised he was holding a small gun in his hand.

'How the hell is this meant to play out, Edward? What can you achieve from all of this now?'

'There's always another move to make, Mrs Grayson, always. I want to talk, just you and me. You and your family are incredibly persistent.'

'Where's Lucia?'

'I'll show you in a moment. For now, listen to me. We can work this out. Nobody else has to die today.'

'It's over, Edward, can't you see that? You've lost. You're surrounded by police. Unless you've got a bloody great plan, your career as MP is finished.'

'I want you to come here and look out of the window

behind me. I think that will help to focus your mind. We have five, maybe ten minutes now to come up with a plan. One thing you need to be very certain of is that I will not be spending any time in jail. Either we agree to something right now, or none of us leaves this platform alive.'

'Where's Lucia, you piece of shit?' Charlotte yelled.

Edward waved out of the window with his hand. At the back of the container lift was a huge supporting iron girder. It served no function other than to provide the framework on which the structure's mechanisms were based. It had no protective railings and no gangplanks. It was totally exposed. And on her hands and knees in the middle of it, looking scared beyond sanity and fighting to maintain her balance in the wind, was Lucia.

CHAPTER THIRTY-NINE

Morecambe - Present Day

'It helps to focus the mind, doesn't it?' Edward said, his voice cold.

'You're a monster!' Charlotte screamed at him. She started to move towards him, her fists clenched, but he raised the gun.

'That's far enough.'

Charlotte stopped dead, her anger turning to tears.

'I'm a businessman, Charlotte, so let's talk business. You've caused me considerable problems during the past week, and it's time we settled this thing between us.'

'I don't understand what this is all about. Why is my family caught up in this? Lucia is still a child.'

Charlotte was staying close to the window to keep Lucia in her sight. If she'd been scared when she'd seen her bound and gagged in the old paddling pool at the abandoned holiday camp, now she was verging on a panic attack. One wrong move, one slip, and Lucia would hurtle to the

242 PAUL J. TEAGUE

ground below, striking several iron supports on the way down.

'I've been trying to work it out myself, to be honest with you,' Edward continued. 'We finally got the answer from your friend in Fletcher Prison, Jenna Phillips. That woman is to blame for all of this. If she'd have come clean with us in 1984 – or in 2006 come to that - this might have all been averted.'

'Bruce Craven!'

Charlotte almost spat out the words. She wished Bruce were still alive, so she could tear out his eyes. How could one person cause such trouble?

'Yes, the ubiquitous Bruce Craven. I wish to God I'd never met that man.'

Charlotte checked Lucia. She would need to draw this to whatever conclusion Edward was seeking, and fast.

'You and me both. But he's dead. You know that, don't you? Jenna told you that. You abducted her daughter, for Christ's sake. Wasn't that enough?'

'But she never told us about you and your husband, did she? Not until our prison guard in Fletcher Prison strung her up in her cell and almost choked the life out of her. She's a tough cookie, that one. Protected you right to the end.'

Charlotte wanted to be sick, remembering how quick she'd been to judge her former friend. She'd been furious that Jenna had tried to extort cash from them, but she'd kept her mouth shut, at huge personal cost. It was all too much to take in.

Edward gave her an intimidating stare. 'You understand I can't let you speak to the police, don't you? You know too much now. If you hadn't gone chasing after us with that tin-pot reporter from the local paper, we might have been able to find a way out of this.'

'It's over, Edward. Do you know about Daisy Bowker? I'll bet you don't. She's Bruce's half-sister, she's aware he disappeared, and she won't let it drop. Bruce Craven was like a disease. He infected all of us. You can't stop this now; the truth has to come out. You can't keep killing everybody.'

Edward's expression changed. He clearly wasn't aware of Daisy Bowker.

'Daisy Bowker can be sorted...'

'And what about the videos? I haven't seen them, but Rex Emery reckons there's evidence on them that will send your entire pack of cards tumbling. Did you know I stole them from your house earlier? That tin-pot reporter you mentioned picked them up from your garden a short time ago and then called the police. It's finished, Edward. Let's end this without any more deaths.'

Charlotte looked out at Lucia again. She was beginning to shiver now in the icy wind. Charlotte willed her daughter not to look down.

Close your eyes, Lucia. Hold on tight. I'm coming for you.

Edward now looked furious. She'd wrong-footed him.

'Who filmed those videos, Edward? Where did they come from? Surely a man as careful as you wouldn't be so careless.'

'I don't know where those videos came from, but when I find out, I'll—'

'What, Edward? You'll arrange for somebody else to be killed? How many people have to die to keep your silly little secrets? Is it worth it?'

Charlotte wanted to scream at Edward Callow, but she

stopped herself. If she pushed him too hard, she might place Lucia in further danger.

'You said you wanted to strike a deal?'

Edward looked out of the window, checking on Lucia.

'Yes. You can have your daughter, and I promise to protect you. You must get those videos back to me and tell the police your daughter was suicidal. They don't even know I'm here yet—'

Charlotte thought it unlikely. Nigel Davies should have imparted that information when he phoned DCI Summers. Callow didn't need to know that. She should play along. If it got her to Lucia faster, she'd tell whatever lies were necessary.

Edward was thinking aloud. 'We'll blame the recent deaths on Bob Moseley and Neil Carthy. I assume they're dead too?' he said.

Charlotte nodded.

'What about that idiot, Tyler?' Edward asked

'He's locked up in the container where you tried to kill Rex Emery.'

'Leave him in there. He'll die eventually. You know he formed a relationship with your daughter? The fool was only supposed to get information from her at the arcade. I should think we'll both be pleased to see him dead.'

There it was again, that surging mix of anger, guilt, sadness and powerlessness. Sometimes Charlotte felt so useless as a mother. She'd let Lucia down.

'So, I rescue Lucia, we walk down the steps, and you hide out until it's safe to sneak out of the docks? What about the cars you used?'

'You don't think they're registered to me, do you?'

'How do you know I won't rescue Lucia, then hand you over to the police?'

'I don't,' Edward replied. 'But you saw what I did to your friend Jenna in prison. If I get locked away, I will have my revenge, Charlotte. Do you want to be looking over your shoulder for the rest of your life? It seems to me you've been doing that long enough already.'

Charlotte realised how this was playing out. Edward Callow had no intention of letting her and Lucia out alive. And she had no intention of allowing this madman to walk away.

'Why now, Edward? Where did all of this come from?'

She didn't expect an answer.

'Because I want to retire,' Edward said. 'Not from politics, but from my past. I wanted to tidy things up, erase the errors of my former life and then try for prime minister. I was cleaning up, that's all. I want to move on with my life.'

'I agree to your terms,' Charlotte said. 'Let me get Lucia. We'll walk from here. You can hide up in the cab like a five-year-old until they clear the area. If they find you, I'll tell them you were helping me talk down Lucia. I promise. I want to retire too, Edward. I want this done. For me, my family, Piper, and Rex.'

Edward waved the gun.

'Go. Get your daughter.'

'As simple as that?' Charlotte asked. She didn't trust him for one moment.

'As simple as that,' he replied.

Charlotte glanced out of the far window again. She had to act now. Moving towards the door of the cab, she didn't take her eyes off Edward. She suspected he might make a move, but she didn't know what it would be.

She crept on to the platform and moved toward the rear of the cab. The wind was icy and fierce; Lucia's hands and fingers would seize up. If she didn't get her off that supporting pillar soon, she wouldn't be able to hold on much longer.

Charlotte could see the helicopter still circling the harbour area. Even at that height, she was able to hear activity and voices on the ground below her. She stepped around the far side of the cab and saw Lucia, completely exposed, hanging on to the post with both hands, the sleeves of her top pulled down to gain what little protection against the cold she could. Her back was to Charlotte; Edward must have forced her to crawl out there with the gun pointed at her. Another bully, like Bruce Craven.

Charlotte walked up to the iron support, which was protected only by a small barrier. The chances of surviving a fall were minimal, despite Edward's threat of Lucia ending up crippled. Not too far below was a container, suspended from the lift's chain mechanism. It looked like whoever was last on shift had given up moving the container half-way through a manoeuvre.

Charlotte looked down one more time, then across at Lucia.

'Lucia, darling, I'm here. Hold on. I'm coming to get you.'

CHAPTER FORTY

Morecambe - Present Day

As she stepped out on the iron girder, Charlotte realised she'd seriously lost track of what was going on outside while she'd been in the cab with Edward. Of course, the helicopter had spotted Lucia already, but it was keeping a distance, circling wide. Most of the police activity was now focused at the base of the container lift. It was almost over now.

'Mum, I can't move. I can't feel my hands. I'm going to fall, I know it.'

Charlotte was still clutching the barrier, dreading taking the next step without something to hold on to. The supporting girder was wider than her two feet placed slightly apart. It had a lip on it, which meant Lucia could at least hang on to it. It was precarious and exposed; but it was possible. The wind didn't help, icy cold as it blew off the sea, beating against her body.

'I'm coming out to get you, Lucia. Hold on. We'll walk back together—'

'He's got a gun, Mum. He'll shoot us. I'm so sorry... I didn't mean this to happen.'

Lucia needed to stay calm. Charlotte thought back to when she was a toddler, terrified of seeing the dentist. She would distract her, as she used to do then.

'It doesn't matter, Lucia. I'm here now. We'll be home soon, with Dad and Olli. It won't be long. Remember that holiday we were talking about? How about we get it booked as soon as we're back home, nice and warm?'

She let go of the barrier and started to edge along the girder. The helicopter was above her, coming in fairly close, the force from its blades making her wobble. She stepped back and grasped the barrier, trying to avoid using her left arm.

'Keep away!' she screamed, waving her hand at the pilot.

'Edward Callow, this is the police—'

They had a loudspeaker system in the helicopter. They knew Edward was up there. That might change things. With the helicopter at a safer distance now, she released her grip on the barrier and began to step out towards Lucia.

'Are they coming for us, Mum?'

'It'll be over soon, darling.'

'Please move out to the platform with your hands in the air—'

The voice of the police officer in the helicopter could be heard clearly, despite the noise of the blades and the wind whipping around her ears.

'What do you think, Spain or France?' Charlotte continued, trying to ignore everything that was going on. Let the police deal with Edward Callow. Her priority was Lucia.

Lucia was sobbing.

'Spain, Mum. It's warmer than France. I want to be somewhere warm—'

Charlotte was a metre or so out from the barrier. Her head swam as she looked at the ground below her, the police officers on the ground terrifyingly small. She straightened her head, focusing on Lucia. Her daughter was three to four metres away. The further she went from the barrier, the more exposed she felt. How must Lucia feel?

'Hold tight, Lucia, hold tight. I know it's scary, but so long as you stay still and hold tight, you'll be fine. Just imagine Spain. I promise, the first thing we'll do when we're home will be to book that holiday, okay?'

'Come any nearer, and I'll shoot both of them!'

Charlotte's instinct was to look, but if she did, she'd lose her balance and fall. She followed Lucia's lead, crouching slowly, ignoring the pain in her left arm, placing her knees gently on the iron support and clasping the sides with her hands. The metalwork was startlingly cold. It was unforgiving against her knees, but it was her arm that was causing the biggest problem. She fought through the pain, turning her head carefully to assess the situation.

The helicopter had pulled away sharply. Edward was pressed tight against the exterior of the cab, waving his gun towards them both.

'Mr Callow, please place the gun on the floor and your hands where we can see them clearly.'

There was a marksman in that helicopter, but would they take out an MP? Even one brandishing a gun?

The suspended container was about two metres beyond where Lucia was kneeling. Seeing it closer up made it possible to get a sharper sense of the distances involved. Could they jump down to it? Was this a way out?

'Lucia, I need you to trust me. Remember when you were a little girl, and I told you the dentist was a nice lady and she wouldn't hurt you? And you didn't trust me until it was over?'

Lucia sobbed her reply.

'Yes, Mum. She was a great dentist. It didn't hurt a bit.'

'I need you to move forward, further out towards the end of the girder—'

'No, Mum, I can't!'

'Lucia, trust me. I need you to be braver than you've ever been in your life. Can you do that for me?'

'I'm so scared, mum. My hands are frozen. I don't think I can move—'

'Keep away, or I'll shoot both of them!'

Edward's voiced sounded deranged as he screamed at the helicopter, which was now keeping its distance.

A shot rang out. Charlotte felt nothing, and Lucia seemed to be okay. She gripped the sides of the girder and looked behind her. Edward was shooting at the police below. They must have taken positions along the stairways leading up to the platform at the top.

'Just edge forward. You don't have to open your eyes. Feel your way. Hold on tight. I'll tell you when to stop.'

Lucia was moving now, and Charlotte was closing in on her daughter. The police would soon be there. She tried to blank out Edward's voice behind her. He sounded insane, a megalomaniac whose time was nearly up.

Charlotte could sense the helicopter moving near them. They had to be seeking an angle to take out Edward Callow. But would he get to them before the police took their shot?

'Just a little further now, Lucia. You can do it.'

There was a loud, metallic clank below Charlotte. She

felt the vibration in the girder and tensed up. A terrible pain shot through her left-hand side again.

Lucia was there now. They were out of time; Callow was shooting at them. It was jump or be shot.

She wanted the police to bring the helicopter in close and shoot him. But if they did, the force from the blades would blow her and Lucia off the girder. Maybe they'd figured that out.

'You have to stand up now, Lucia—'

'I can't, Mum. My knees have seized up from being here so long—'

'Please Lucia, just do it.'

There was another ricochet off the side of the girder, this time closer to Lucia. She jumped, flinched and almost fell. Her hands grasped at the edges again, and she steadied herself. Charlotte's heart almost flew out of her mouth as she watched.

'Please, Lucia. Stand up. Then open your eyes and look carefully below you. You'll have to jump. I'll follow you—'

Lucia was sobbing wildly now, but she did as she was told.

Another bullet was fired. The helicopter swooped in closer, then pulled back as Charlotte waved them away, feeling the force from the blades.

'You can do it, Lucia. Jump down on the top of the container, and you'll be safe. I'll follow you. It looks high, but it's okay, I swear—'

Before she had time to finish her sentence, Lucia had jumped. Charlotte watched as her daughter plummeted through the air momentarily, then landed right in the middle of the container's roof. She could hear Lucia half-crying, half-laughing at the sheer relief of it.

'You stupid, fucking bitch,' Edward Callow shouted.

Charlotte gripped on tightly and looked back. Edward was growing frustrated. He was standing by the barrier at the end of the girder, looking crazy with frustration that his shots had missed, his eyes wild and fiery. He levelled up his gun and aimed it at Charlotte, taking his time as though he had no intention of missing.

Charlotte faced forwards again and saw Lucia standing on the roof of the container, clutching one of the chains it was suspended from, urging her mother to jump.

It was no good; she was too far away from the container, yet she could sense Edward aiming the weapon, intent on killing her before the police got to him.

She'd had enough of evil men wrecking their life, threatening her family. Charlotte looked ahead at the container below her and stood up cautiously. A shot sounded, and a bullet whooshed at her side. Her left arm was on fire with the pain from the dislocation, but she ignored it. She had one chance at this; one opportunity to join her daughter and see her husband and son again.

Charlotte jumped towards the container below her, using up her last reserves of energy. If she missed, she'd crash on to the concrete below. At least Lucia, Olli and Will were safe.

As she made her leap, Charlotte heard two gunshots. One came from Edward's direction and the other came from somewhere else, she couldn't tell where.

As she fell, she realised she couldn't make it. She was going to land short.

CHAPTER FORTY-ONE

Morecambe - Present Day

The digger was too loud to make himself heard, so Will moved further away, followed by DCI Summers.

'You're certain that's where he is?' she asked.

'It was well over thirty years ago, DCI Summers. But yes, I'm as sure as I can be.'

'They'll find him if he's there. It's a good job they haven't built on top of it yet.'

Will leaned against what remained of the arcade wall. So many years had passed, and so many memories. And Charlotte, his beautiful Charlotte... this was where it had all begun. Two teenagers, naïve and in love, at the start of their lives together, and now with two beautiful children. He was so proud of Olli and Lucia and how they'd coped in the aftermath of that night. They were growing up; they'd soon be moving on and making their own lives. He hoped they would find a love like his and Charlotte's, one that had weathered so many storms.

Will looked around. Large houses now stood where the chalets had once been, with a newly laid asphalt road through the middle of the old site. On one side of it was the new development, and on the other side, the ghostly remains of a once vibrant holiday camp, awaiting demolition. He could still hear echoes of laughter, of children having fun in the paddling pool, adults telling jokes, dogs running everywhere and loving the mayhem of it all.

The digger stopped, and there was a sudden flurry of activity where the blade had been cutting through the newly broken soil.

'Looks like they've found something,' DCI Summers said. 'Daisy Bowker will be pleased. I think we're all owed answers.'

Will swallowed hard. It was hard to believe that it had been thirty-five years since that night. He could still recall the terror of it, fearful that he'd killed Bruce Craven. He was only a kid back then, like Lucia and Olli, ignorant about the world and scared out of his wits that he'd killed a man, even if it was in self-defence. He'd kept that secret to himself for so many years and look where it ended. Poor Charlotte. They should have told the truth back then. Even if they'd thought Bruce was alive and had left the holiday camp, they should have reported it to the police.

The camp was almost gone now, and in another year, the last of the ruins would be cleared and there would be houses on both sides of the road. Good riddance to it. But he still had his happy memories. He'd think about those and forget about Bruce Craven now. That evil man had ruined enough lives already.

A police officer wearing a fluorescent top walked over to DCI Summers and nodded at her.

'That's it, ma'am, we've found bones.'

EPILOGUE

Morecambe - Present Day

The lounge had never looked brighter. Large clusters of brightly coloured balloons decorated each corner of the room, streamers criss-crossed from one side to the other, and the tables were set with champagne bottles and glasses. There were sandwiches, cakes and party-poppers. It appeared to be the craziest gathering ever, as if the host couldn't decide what they were celebrating: *Welcome Home* and *Congratulations* banners were stuck on the walls.

There was a round of applause as Will wheeled Charlotte into the room. For a moment, she was overcome with emotion; the sight of Olli and Lucia there, their faces lit up at her arrival, was almost more than she could bear. Will began to address the small gathering.

'I'll only bore you for a few moments,' he began.

Charlotte looked up at him and smiled.

'A few minutes? That'll be the day!'

There was laughter, and Will carried on. Charlotte didn't care. She'd be happy to listen to that voice forever.

'We're here to celebrate several things this afternoon. I don't want to dwell on the past. Let today be all about the future. First and foremost, my wife is home. And the good news is, she'll be out of this chair in no time; in fact, she's already able to use a stick.'

There was another round of applause.

Charlotte realised how lucky she was. A momentary surge of panic overcame her as she recalled those final moments: how she'd narrowly missed the container, smashing the bones in her leg as she clipped the side, but caught one of the chains with her right hand. How she'd struggled to secure her grip with her left hand, but hadn't been able to raise herself up because of the unbearable pain from the dislocation. And how her daughter, so young and fragile, had found the courage to reach out to her mother. She'd lifted her up to safety, as Edward Callow's body tumbled from the side of the huge container lift, struck by the bullet of a police marksman who'd seized her moment the second Charlotte was out of the way and she had a clear shot.

Sure, Charlotte needed rehabilitation and some metal components fitting into her leg to bring it all back together again. And she'd always have some discomfort in her left arm, according to the doctor. But she was alive. Her family was safe; they'd all made it out of there. She considered it a small price to pay. It was a massive relief to see her friends all gathered there. Her panic was soon replaced with relief and gratitude.

'We're also here to celebrate George's all-clear from cancer. It was a close call there, my friend, you had us all worried. I can't tell you how delighted we all are, George. We love you and Isla dearly; you're like family to us.'

Una barked, prompting laughter and another round of applause.

'I have some good news myself. Normally, I'd keep quiet about it, but today of all days, this is about moving towards the future—'

Charlotte looked around the room. She'd seen the kids, George and Isla standing at the front, Una with her tail wagging furiously, Nigel Davies and Willow too. But she'd missed the three women sitting in the far corner of the room; Abi Smithson, Daisy Bowker and Abi's daughter, Louise, all together, enjoying each other's company.

Will had told her about the trio meeting when he'd visited her in hospital, and she was so pleased. At last, Daisy had found out everything about her half-brother, and she was horrified when the truth came out. Will had suggested to Abi that letting Daisy know about Bruce's child might help to heal more wounds. Abi had agreed, reluctantly, according to Will, but it looked like things had worked out well while she'd been recovering in Lancaster Infirmary. The three women were obviously comfortable in each other's company.

'Finally,' Will continued, 'I get my own pat on the back. I finally got a job at Lancaster University and handed in my notice yesterday. We're all getting the fresh start that we deserve.'

There was a call for three cheers from George, then everybody moved off into huddles, chatting away and drinking the champagne that Olli and Willow were now distributing.

Lucia walked over to Charlotte, bent down and put her

arms around her mother. The two of them began to cry, laughing at themselves for being so daft.

'I'm so proud of you, Lucia,' Charlotte said. 'You never have to apologise to me. I'm your mother, and I'll always be here for you, whatever happens to you from now on.'

She pulled Lucia in tight, wanting the moment to last forever. Lucia kissed Charlotte, then went off to fuss Una.

Nigel Davies had been waiting for his moment.

'Good to see you, Charlotte.'

Charlotte wiped her eyes and smiled at him.

'You'd make a great reporter,' he smiled back. 'That was quite an adventure you had.'

'Thanks for getting those videos and alerting the police. You didn't do so badly yourself.'

'It's all sewn up, though I still don't know who recorded that video and where the mystery photos of Isla and George came from. But one thing's clear: Edward Callow's voice is on that video clearly plotting Piper's abduction. It will give the police all the evidence they need.'

Charlotte noticed that there was a momentary lull in the conversation, then it picked up again. DCI Summers had walked into the room, dressed for work. She approached Charlotte.

'I get heart palpitations every time I see you two together,' she said with a grin. Charlotte hadn't seen her smile much since she'd known her, but it lit up her face when she did.

'Any news on Rex Emery?' Nigel asked.

'Well, that's why I wanted to call in briefly,' DCI Summers answered. 'I have some positive news. Rex Emery looks like he'll get a full pardon and possibly damages. It's looking positive for Jenna too. Her case is getting a full review. She'll remain in custody for the time being, but she's in a much better facility now and getting the help she needs. If you asked me to place a bet on it, I think she'll walk free. She's helped considerably in putting the pieces together in this whole sorry tale. And did you know she's been reunited with her daughter, Piper?'

'I'd heard that from Olli,' Charlotte answered. 'I'd hoped Piper and her friend Agnieszka might be here today. I want to offer them work at the guest house. I'm convinced now she and Jenna are two more of Bruce Craven's victims. Jenna did an amazing thing protecting my family, even if she showed terrible judgement in that crackpot scheme she thought up with Pat Harris. I want to help her and Piper make things right. I want Jenna to get her life back.'

DCI Summers nodded.

'I can't stay long,' she said, 'I'll say hello to Will, then be on my way. It's great to see you back, Charlotte. That was some rescue. I hope your daughter is very proud of you.'

'Do you know why Edward Callow had those photographs of Isla and George?' Charlotte asked. She'd been unable to figure it out.

'We think it was just part of an ongoing surveillance operation being carried out by Callow. And that Tyler chap, the one with the Mohican; he's more than keen to confirm that Edward sent him out to tail Isla, now he's trying to reduce his prison sentence. I'm sure we'll get more information from him as his case progresses through the courts. Oh, and that audio you recorded on your phone; it will all help piece this together.'

'What about the deaths of Barry McMillan and Mason Jones?' Nigel asked. 'I take they ended their lives because they knew the game was up?'

'We think so,' DCI Summers continued. 'We never found McMillan's phone, but we assume Edward was threatening to release that picture of them with the girl. We may never be able to confirm that, but it seems most likely. The shame of everybody finding out probably drove them to do it.'

DCI Summers and Nigel walked off, leaving Charlotte with her own thoughts.

She looked towards the large window at the front of the lounge. Isla was sitting on her own, tears dampening her cheeks. She seemed keen to hide it, but she was failing. Charlotte wheeled her chair over to her. She still hadn't got the hang of the thing. She'd be pleased when she could walk properly again.

'What's up, Isla? Why the sad face?'

'I'm happy, honestly,' Isla replied. 'I'm so pleased everything turned out fine, Charlotte. You got your family back, and that's the most important thing on earth.'

'And George got the all-clear, his treatment has been successful. Everything's good, Isla. We can all look to the future now.'

'I was thinking about my first husband, Richard, and my son, Philip. I never talk about them, but I think about them every day—'

'I'm so sorry, Isla. I wish you'd told us. That was a terrible thing to happen. You should have shared it with us. We've all been hurt by those men. It's terrible what happened to your husband and son.'

'I always loved this job because I could see them coming home in the boat after a morning's fishing. I'd stand in this window and look out to the bay, relieved they were home. After they died, after my depression, and when Rex had gone, I came back to work here. It gave me comfort to look out to sea. I'd imagine that nothing had changed, that they were sailing back every day, safe and sound.'

Charlotte put her hand on Isla's arm and gave it a gentle squeeze.

'Thank you for being brave, Charlotte,' Isla said after a few moments silence. 'I'm sorry I held back from telling you the truth.'

'What do you mean?'

'That I knew about Rex Emery. And Piper. It was me who made that video of those men. I hid a camera among the bottles of the bar. I was aware something was going on, what with their private meetings and that horrible man, Harvey Turnbull. When Edward Callow caught me snooping around, I thought I was a dead woman. And I sent those photos to Nigel Davies too. I thought you two would figure it out between you. The photographer, Rory Higson, gave me copies years ago, I asked him to, just in case they came in useful later. My instincts were right, I never trusted those men, even in the early days before Piper was abducted. After what happened at Adventure Kingdom, I was too scared to do anything about it. But when Barry McMillan died, I realised it was time, after all those years. When I noticed you and Nigel chatting at Barry's book launch event that evening, I thought to myself, those two make a great a team. I'm pleased my instincts were right.'

'Why didn't you do anything with the video?' Charlotte asked. 'You could have brought those men down years ago.'

'You've seen what they were like. They would stop at nothing. I still have a sister and brother in the area. When they made me watch Harvey Turnbull's death, I was terrified, Charlotte. They frightened me so much, I kept quiet and got on with my life. But it was me who sent the video to Piper Phillips when those men started dying. It was me who delivered those photos to Nigel Davies at the newspaper offices, in the hope he'd piece it all together. Una likes her early morning walks, it gave me a good excuse to be out walking early. But I didn't have your courage all those years ago, when I was your age, Charlotte—'

'I'm no hero, Isla. I just did what anybody would do in the same situation.'

'You're my hero, Charlotte. And I'm sure Will, Olli, Lucia, Rex, Piper, Jenna... all those people will tell you the same thing. You found the courage to fight when the rest of us cowered. You were the first to strike that man Bruce Craven with a stone. And now he really is dead, Charlotte. And that's all because of you.'

Charlotte's adventures continue in the second Morecambe Bay Trilogy, which is available now in paperback and e-book formats.

AUTHOR NOTES

So come on, admit it: you must have wondered if Charlotte and Lucia were going to make it out of there alive, just for a minute?

I hope you enjoyed reading that ending as much as I enjoyed writing it and that you felt all the loose ends got tied up nicely.

When I write exciting scenes like that, my typing gets faster and faster. I can't wait to get the words down.

So that's it, the Morecambe Bay trilogy is now concluded.

I can't tell you how much fun it was writing this series. It's been a great trip down memory lane for me.

I hope my love of the resort shines through; I managed to squeeze in some more of the resort's fabulous locations in this story.

Firstly, there's Heysham Port, which I had to revisit on a research trip before publishing the book.

My only memory of visiting it was as a trainee journalist, when a friend and I were recording video news reports to cut our teeth as TV reporters.

All I can remember is that we put our poor interviewee through his paces only to get to the end of the session and find that nothing had recorded.

My career as a journalist could only go uphill from there.

I've fictionalised the port. It's much like any other port, with a ferry terminal, a railway stop, car parking and various fenced-off areas for lorries.

In my story, the port is a little more heavy-duty than in real life, but sometimes you have to embellish things a little to make them work better in a thriller scenario.

I've never been to the Regent Bay Holiday Park, but I've passed it many a time, and I harbour a secret love of static caravan parks, as is evidenced in my Don't Tell Meg trilogy, in book 2.

So it's a fictional Regent Bay Holiday Park in this story, but it feels like the kind of place Steven Terry and Abi Smithson would appear at.

We also make a move to Lancaster in this book.

I spent 1983-1991 living in Lancaster, as a student and a primary school teacher. I also met my wife at the college and we married in the city.

The bus station is portrayed as it was in 1984, before the redevelopment, and The Merchants pub, where Will and Charlotte take refuge for a short time, remains open.

It's based in a series of old, stone cellar-like structures and is a must-visit location if you're in the city.

Finally, we have Fletcher Prison, a fictional location which is closely modelled on Styal Prison in Cheshire.

I was moved by the story told in an old documentary and wanted to reflect some of the prison's issues in my story.

I hope you believe that Jenna got a fair outcome at the end of the story; she certainly deserves it.

I had an interesting challenge when writing this book, and it caused me considerable head-scratching.

Left for Dead was mainly Charlotte's story, with a bit of Jenna and Will added too.

I wanted this final book to take place over the course of one night, much as my standalone thriller Dead of Night does.

However, I had to give Charlotte time to recover after her considerable trials at the end of Circle of Lies.

I decided to do that by handing over part of the story to Will; it gave us all a good chance to get to know him a little better too.

Shall I let you into a secret?

George was going to die at the end of the story, but I couldn't bring myself to do it, it was just too bleak.

And after revealing Isla's terrible back story, I decided to give her a break.

Watch out next time, George; you never know who's for the chop next!

I hope you got to know Edward Callow a little better too in this story.

I was interested in showing how a man turns bad during a period of three decades, at first trying to better himself, but ultimately becoming another of the megalomaniacs he once despised.

Edward gets what he deserves; he's a nasty man and will stop at nothing to build his empire of power.

I need to point out that all schools referred to in this story are fictional.

Morecambe does have an academy, but for the record, my story does not feature it.

My thriller is a fusion of fact and fiction. Sometimes it seems unfair to feature real-life locations in a murder story, so I have intentionally avoided doing that in this trilogy.

In a small town like Morecambe, it's also important to point out for legal reasons that this story is fictional, and all characters are made up.

If you live in the UK, you may have watched The Bay TV series.

It's what prompted me to write Left for Dead in the first place.

Seeing all those lovely Morecambe Bay locations brought lots of memories flooding back; do give it a try if you can get it from your TV provider.

I'm delighted that early feedback on Left for Dead frequently mentions how much readers love reading about the locations in Morecambe and hearing how the resort changed over the years, in between 1984 and the present day.

If you love your crime and thriller books and you like the sound of Morecambe, why not check out the rather excellent crime festival that takes place there every year?

It's called Morecambe and Vice, and I recommend it to all lovers of crime fiction.

So, that's it for the Morecambe Bay trilogy.

But I feel that these characters still have more adventures in them.

If you'd like to hear more from Charlotte, Will, Olli, Lucia, George, Nigel and Una, please drop me a line to let me know.

If you'd like to see DCI Kate Summers and Steven Terry in a different adventure, I'd recommend the Don't Tell Meg trilogy as your next read.

If you like your UK seaside resorts, much of that book is

set in Blackpool, and you'll get a real sense of the British seaside in that story too.

You'll find several image galleries and links to Morecambe websites over at https://paulteague.net, the home of my thriller books written under Paul J. Teague.

If you liked this story and want to stay in touch, I'll be delighted if you register for my email updates at https://paulteague.net/thrillers, as that's where I share news of what I'm writing and tell you about any reader discounts and freebies that are available.

Paul Teague

ALSO BY PAUL J. TEAGUE

Morecambe Bay Trilogy 1

Book 1 - Left For Dead

Book 2 - Circle of Lies

Book 3 - Truth Be Told

Morecambe Bay Trilogy 2

Book 4 - Trust Me Once

Book 5 - Fall From Grace

Book 6 - Bound By Blood

Morecambe Bay Trilogy 3

Book 7 - First To Die

Book 8 - Nothing To Lose

Book 9 - Last To Tell

Note: The Morecambe Bay trilogies are best read in the order shown above.

Don't Tell Meg Trilogy

Features DCI Kate Summers and Steven Terry.

Book 1 - Don't Tell Meg

Book 2 - The Murder Place

Book 3 - The Forgotten Children

Standalone Thrillers

Dead of Night

One Last Chance

No More Secrets

So Many Lies

Two Years After

Friends Who Lie

Now You See Her

ABOUT THE AUTHOR

Hi, I'm Paul Teague, the author of the Morecambe Bay series and the Don't Tell Meg trilogy, as well as several other standalone psychological thrillers such as One Last Chance, Dead of Night and No More Secrets.

I'm a former broadcaster and journalist with the BBC, but I have also worked as a primary school teacher, a disc jockey, a shopkeeper, a waiter and a sales rep.

I've read thrillers all my life, starting with Enid Blyton's Famous Five series as a child, then graduating to James Hadley Chase, Harlan Coben, Linwood Barclay and Mark Edwards.

Let's get connected!
https://paulteague.net

Lightning Source UK Ltd.
Milton Keynes UK
UKHW010400180223
417178UK00002B/265

9 781916 475120